Ginger Snapped

Copyright © 2025 by Patti Petrone Miller
All rights reserved.
No part of this publication may be reproduced, stored in a retrieval system, or transmitted in any form or by any means—electronic, mechanical, photocopying, recording, or otherwise—without the prior written permission of the author, except in the case of brief quotations embodied in reviews, articles, or scholarly analysis.

This is a work of fiction. Names, characters, places, and incidents are either the product of the author's imagination or used fictitiously. Any resemblance to actual persons, living or dead, events, or locales is entirely coincidental.

Publisher: AP Miller Productions
ISBN: 9798282905670

Cover Design by: PIXEL SQUIRREL

Printed in the United States of America

For more information, visit: https://pattipetrone-miller.com/

First Edition: November 2024

Patti Petrone Miller

Excerpt from Ginger Snapped by Patti Petrone Miller

The brass bell above the bakery door jingled its usual cheerful tune, but the chill that followed was anything but comforting. Ginger glanced up from the counter where she was piping cranberry glaze onto her gingerbread scones. A manila envelope, worn at the edges and damp from the snow, had been slid beneath the door.

No note. No sender.

Heart thudding like a mixer on high speed, she peeled it open with flour-dusted fingers. Inside were grainy photographs—blown-up images from security footage. One showed the alley behind Ginger Snaps Bakery. The next: a gloved hand reaching for the dumpster.

The third photo made her stomach drop. It was Edith Fernwood, unmistakably alive, stepping out from the back door of the bakery—hours after Ginger had locked up.

"What in the world…" she whispered.

The door creaked behind her. She whirled around, nearly smearing the glaze across her apron.

It was Detective Dan Griffith.

"I was hoping we could talk," he said, his eyes scanning the photos still clutched in her hands. "Looks like someone beat me to it."

Ginger's breath caught in her throat. "Dan, if Edith was here after I left—what does that mean?"

He stepped closer, his voice low, steady. "It means someone wanted her to be found here. And they're making sure you take the fall."

Ginger Snapped

Authors Book List

Accidental Vows
A Very Merry Krampus Christmas
A Devil's Bargain
The Devilf of London
Sin Takes A Holiday
Barking Up The Wrong Bakery, Thankgiving
Barking Up The Wrong Bakery, Christmas
Best Served Dead
Bewitching Charms
Christmas at Hollybrook Inn
Christmas on Peppermit Lane
Cabinet of Curiosities
Krampus
Hex and the City
Love in Stitches
Pies and Perps
Spectres and Souffles
Mamma Mia It's Murder
Once Upon A Christmas
The Fatman
The Frosted Felony
The Purr-fect Suspect
The Boogeyman
The Gingerdead Men
Vikings Enchantress
Welcome to Scarecrow Hollow
The Pendleton Witches
Christmas In Pine Haven
Love in the Stacks
Once Upon A Christmas
Frosted Felony
Truth or Dare
Before the Fire
Heart of the Beast
Savage Bloodline
The Secret Ingredient, Mad Batter Bakery Mysteries Prequel

Patti Petrone Miller

Drive By Pies, Mad Batter Bakery Mysteries book 1
Venom in Vanilla, The Sundae of Secrets Series
A Scoop of Murder
Blood Moon Justice
Hot Flashes and Homicide
Crochet Carnage
Hooked By Crooks
The Big Bad
Blood Moon Justice
My Soul to Keep
Murder in the Throne Room
Snowed Inn
Murder on the Menu, A Taste for Trouble Series Book 1
Crumb and Punishment, A Taste For Trouble Series Book 2
Grounds for Murder, A Taste for Trouble Series Book 3
Frosted With Fear, Deadly Delights Series Book 1

GINGER SNAPPED

Patti Petrone Miller

Praise For Author "Patti Petrone Miller's books hit different from your typical feel-good stories. Sure, Hallmark's got their formula down pat, but Miller brings something fresh to the table - authentic characters that actually feel like people you know, dealing with real-life stuff while still keeping things wonderfully uplifting.
I honestly get the same warm fuzzies reading her books as I do curling up with hot cocoa for a Hallmark marathon, but without all the predictable plot points we've seen a million times. She's nailed that sweet spot between heartwarming and genuine that's super hard to find these days. If you're looking for stories that'll leave you smiling but don't make you roll your eyes at how perfect everything is, Miller's your girl. She's got that special touch that makes you feel like you're hanging out with friends rather than just reading about characters. Move over, Hallmark - there's a new queen of wholesome in town!"

For Tessa, the greatest love of my life

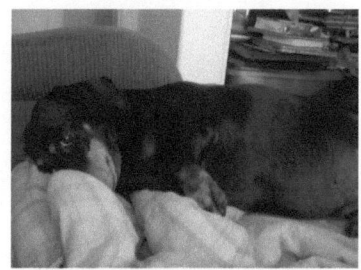

Patti Petrone Miller

Chapter 6

The early morning silence of Haversham Falls was broken only by the gentle hum of Ginger Snaps bakery's industrial ovens and the rhythmic thump of dough hitting the flour-dusted wooden countertop. The aroma of cinnamon and ginger wafted through the cozy shop, mingling with the earthier scents of freshly ground nutmeg and cardamom that Ginger Lawrence had added to her signature recipe. Her hands, strong and sure from years of kneading dough, worked with practiced precision as flour dusted her well-worn canvas apron like the first snowfall of winter.

The worn floorboards beneath her feet creaked with familiar comfort, each board holding memories of the countless steps she'd taken since taking over the bakery. Her mother's old copper mixing bowls gleamed on the open shelving, catching the golden rays of dawn that filtered through the frost-kissed windows. A few stray auburn curls escaped her messy bun, tickling her neck as she hummed an old lullaby her father used to sing – the same one that now often drifted through her dreams of sugared violets and candied roses.

The antique brass bell above the door chimed its melodious greeting, the sound echoing off the exposed brick walls that still held traces of the building's history as Haversham Falls' first general store. Ginger looked up to see her parents entering the shop, bringing with them a gust of crisp December air that made the vintage cookie cutters hanging from iron hooks tinkle like wind chimes.

"There's our girl," Marianne said warmly, her voice carrying the same comforting tone that had soothed Ginger through countless childhood mishaps and teenage heartbreaks. Her mother's pearl earrings – a Lawrence family heirloom – caught the light as she moved, a familiar sight that always made Ginger smile.

The sight of her parents standing in the doorway of her bakery made Ginger's heart swell with an emotion that felt too big for her chest. "Mom, Dad! What are you doing here so early?" The words came out slightly breathless, betraying her surprise and delight.

Nate's eyes crinkled at the corners as he smiled, his weathered hands already reaching for the spare apron hanging on the antique coat rack by the door. The same coat rack that had stood in this spot since 1922, when the building first opened its doors. "Thought you could use an extra set of hands this morning."

"Or two," Marianne added, her fingers already working to tie back her silver-streaked hair. The movement released a hint of her signature lavender perfume – the same scent that had filled their home kitchen throughout Ginger's childhood.

A rush of gratitude warmed Ginger's chest like fresh bread from the oven. "You guys are the best." She gestured toward the mountain of dough waiting to be shaped. "I could definitely use help with the gingerbread men - I've got a big order for the Winter Festival." The annual festival had been a cornerstone of Haversham Falls tradition since the town's founding in 1875, and Ginger felt the weight of responsibility in maintaining its sweetest traditions.

"Say no more," Nate said, rolling up his sleeves to reveal forearms still strong from decades of kneading dough in this very kitchen. The familiar sight brought back memories of watching him work when she was small enough to need a stepping stool to see over the counter.

As they fell into their familiar rhythm, the sweet, spicy scent of freshly baked gingerbread began to fill every corner of the bakery. The recipe was generations old, passed down through the Lawrence family since Ginger's great-grandmother first opened a small bakery stall in the town square. Each batch carried the weight of that history in its perfectly balanced blend of spices.

Ginger watched her father carefully place a perfectly shaped gingerbread man on the well-seasoned baking sheet while her mother skillfully piped intricate patterns of royal icing with the steady hand of an artist. The sight transported her back to countless holiday seasons spent in this very kitchen, learning the secrets of their family recipes one pinch of spice at a time.

The afternoon sun filtered through the bakery's original stained glass transom windows, casting prismatic patterns across the worn wooden floors and illuminating the particles of flour that danced in the air like snow. The vintage clock above the door – salvaged from the old town hall – ticked away the hours as the family worked together, their movements a well-choreographed dance passed down through generations of bakers.

Each person who entered the bakery brought with them their own story, their own connection to the rich tapestry of Haversham Falls history. Mary Ashton, whose grandparents had been among the town's founding families. Neil Bates, whose hardware store had supplied tools to local craftsmen for over sixty years. Nelly Grimes, whose crystal shop occupied the space where the town's first telegraph office once stood.

Together, they created more than just baked goods – they were preserving traditions, building connections, and weaving new stories into the familiar fabric of their small town. As the day drew to a close, the warm glow of the bakery's lights spilled onto Main Street, a beacon of comfort and community in the gathering dusk of a winter evening in Haversham Falls.

The late afternoon brought a new visitor whose presence instantly changed the energy in the room. The bell chimed its welcome as Cara swept in, bringing with her the crisp scent of winter air and pine needles from the Christmas tree lot next door. Her long brown hair, dusted with tiny snowflakes that were just beginning to melt, cascaded down her back like a waterfall of chocolate silk. The sight of her best friend made Ginger's tension ease, as it had since their first day of kindergarten when Cara had shared her rainbow cookies with a shy, red-headed girl who would become her lifelong friend.

"Cara!" Ginger abandoned her task at the counter, leaving a trail of flour footprints as she rushed to embrace her friend. The familiar scent of Cara's vanilla perfume mixed with the bakery's warm, spicy atmosphere, creating a comforting blend that reminded Ginger of countless late-night baking sessions and shared secrets.

"Hey there," Cara laughed, her voice carrying the same musical quality it had when they were children, singing made-up songs about cookies and dreams. She pulled back from the hug, her bright eyes taking in the organized chaos of the holiday rush. "Looks like you've been busy."

The shelves of Ginger Snaps told their own story of the season - gingerbread houses with delicate piping that mimicked the Victorian architecture of Haversham Falls' historic district, sugar cookies cut into shapes of local landmarks, and trays of pies whose recipes dated back to the town's founding. Each treat was more than just food; it was a piece of history, a memory, a tradition passed down through generations of town celebrations and family gatherings.

The warm glow of the vintage pendant lights, salvaged from the old railway station, cast intimate pools of golden light throughout the space. They illuminated the display cases where Ginger's creations sat like edible jewels - glossy chocolate truffles, sugar-dusted pastries, and cookies decorated with such intricate care they looked almost too beautiful to eat. The light caught the copper accents on the walls, making them shimmer like newly minted pennies.

As Cara tied on an apron, its fabric soft and worn from countless washings, Mary Ashton bustled in through the door. The elderly woman's presence brought with it decades of town history - her family had been one of the first to settle in Haversham Falls, and their influence could still be seen in the Georgian architecture of the town square and the meticulously maintained gardens that bloomed in spring.

"Hi, everyone!" Mary's eyes crinkled as she smiled, the wrinkles telling stories of a lifetime of joy and hardship. The brass bell above the door hadn't finished its song before she was enveloped in the warm embrace of fresh-baked comfort. "I hope I'm not interrupting."

Ginger beamed, already reaching for Mary's usual order - a box of assorted pastries that would be shared at tomorrow's garden club meeting. "Not at all, Mary. Your order's almost ready." Her hands moved with practiced efficiency, selecting each pastry with care, knowing exactly which treats would delight each of Mary's friends.

The conversation flowed as naturally as honey, sweet and golden with shared history and mutual affection. They spoke of the upcoming Winter Festival, a tradition that had survived wars, depressions, and changing times. Ginger's planned gingerbread display would feature miniature versions of the town's most beloved landmarks - the old clocktower that still chimed every hour, the covered bridge that had survived the flood of '72, and the gazebo where summer concerts still filled warm evenings with music and laughter.

The arrival of Neil Bates brought with it a different kind of energy - gruff but genuine, like the man himself. His heavy work boots left small puddles of melted snow on the weathered floorboards, and his weathered face carried the perpetual scowl that had become as much a part of town tradition as the cookies he pretended to buy only for his wife.

"Afternoon, Neil," Ginger called out, her voice carrying the warmth that had slowly but surely worn down his grumpy exterior over the years. She already had his usual order - a dozen gingerbread men and a vanilla latte with an extra shot of espresso - ready before he reached the counter.

The bell chimed again, this time announcing the arrival of Nelly Grimes, whose presence transformed the practical space into something almost magical. Her silver hair caught the light like spun moonbeams, tiny crystals woven through the strands creating miniature rainbows that danced on the walls. The jingle of her countless bracelets added a musical accompaniment to her movements, and the subtle scent of sage and jasmine that always surrounded her mixed intriguingly with the bakery's sweet aromas.

"Ah, Ginger, my dear!" Nelly's voice carried the dreamy quality of someone who lived with one foot in this world and one in another, more mystical realm. "I've come to collect the celestial delights you've prepared for my grand reopening."

The cookies Ginger had prepared for Nelly's crystal shop reopening were among her most artistic creations - sugar cookies decorated with intricate celestial patterns, the icing swirled into constellations and galaxies, dusted with edible shimmer that caught the light like real stars. Each one was a tiny edible universe, created with the same care and attention to detail that Nelly brought to selecting her crystals and reading her tarot cards.

As the day progressed, the bakery became more than just a shop - it transformed into a shelter from the growing rumors that had begun to circulate through town, a haven where love and support were as tangible as the treats in the display cases. The weight of unspoken concerns hung in the air like sugar dust, but it was balanced by the strength of community and family bonds that had weathered countless storms before.

Patti Petrone Miller

The phone call from the Haversham Herald brought with it a burst of joy that seemed to make the whole room brighter. Sarah Jennings' request for an interview about Ginger's award-winning gingerbread men felt like validation - not just of her baking skills, but of her place in the community, of the legacy she was continuing.

As the sun began to set, painting the sky in shades of orange and pink that rivaled Ginger's best frosting work, the bakery glowed with warmth and life. The scent of sugar and spice lingered in the air, mixing with the whispered hopes and shared laughter of friends and family. In that moment, surrounded by the people she loved in the place she had always belonged, Ginger felt the truth of what her mother had always said: some ingredients couldn't be measured in cups or spoons – love, tradition, and community were the secret ingredients that made everything sweeter.

The day's final rays of sunlight filtered through the frost-etched windows, casting long shadows across the well-worn floor. These shadows seemed to dance with the spirits of all those who had passed through these doors before - generations of bakers, dreamers, and community members who had made Haversham Falls more than just a spot on a map. It was home, in all its complicated, beautiful, mysterious glory, and Ginger knew that whatever challenges lay ahead, she would face them with the strength of this community behind her, just as sweet and strong as the gingerbread that had brought them all together.

Chapter

The brass key felt ice-cold against Ginger Lawrence's fingers as she unlocked the heavy oak door of Ginger Snaps Bakery. The door's familiar creak echoed through the empty street of Haversham Falls, where even the earliest risers wouldn't appear for another hour. Pre-dawn shadows played across the bakery's vintage storefront, where gold-leafed letters spelled out the shop's name against deep green paint that had weathered twenty Maine winters.

Inhaling deeply, Ginger expected the usual morning symphony of aromas – vanilla, cinnamon, and the lingering sweetness of yesterday's bakes. Instead, the air felt strangely flat. Wrong.

"Another day, another dozen gingerbread men," she murmured her daily mantra, her voice unnaturally loud in the stillness. The words, usually a comfort, felt hollow in the unsettling quiet.

Her fingers found the antique brass light switch, a remnant from when the building had been Haversham Falls' first telephone exchange in 1925. The fluorescent bulbs flickered reluctantly to life, illuminating the cozy space she'd lovingly restored over the past five years. Exposed brick walls displayed black-and-white photographs of the town's history, including one of her grandmother standing proudly before the shop's original opening in 1962.

But something was wrong. The usual morning orchestra of kitchen sounds was absent – no gentle hum of refrigerators, no soft whirr of mixers prepping for the day, no melodic clink of metal bowls and utensils being arranged by Marco, her assistant who always arrived before dawn.

"Marco?" Ginger called out, her voice wavering slightly. "Did you oversleep again?"

Only silence answered.

Her practical shoes – chosen for twelve-hour days standing at the counter – squeaked against the Italian tile floor as she moved deeper into the kitchen. The sound seemed to mock the unusual quiet.

"Get it together, Ging," she chided herself, squaring shoulders that had grown strong from years of kneading dough. "You're just being paranoid. Again. Like that time you thought someone had stolen your mother's recipe book, and it was just stuck behind the flour bins."

But her self-deprecating pep talk did little to calm the unease churning in her stomach. The professional kitchen, usually her haven, felt foreign and threatening in the early morning light.

Ginger's mind raced through her closing routine from the night before. She'd stayed late, perfecting a new gingerbread recipe for the upcoming Winter Festival competition. Every appliance had been running perfectly when she left, each one carefully checked as part of her nightly ritual.

"Maybe there was a power outage," she reasoned aloud, her voice bouncing off the copper pots hanging overhead. The vintage cooking implements, collected from local estate sales, usually gave the kitchen a warm, lived-in feel. Now they looked like sleeping sentinels, watching her every move.

Her hand trembled slightly as she reached for the nearest appliance – a cherry-red industrial mixer that had been her first major investment when she took over the bakery. The power button felt cold under her finger.

"Please work," she whispered, pressing down firmly. The machine remained stubbornly silent.

A chill ran down her spine, raising goosebumps on arms dusted with freckles that matched her copper hair. Something was very wrong here.

"Okay, Lawrence," she told herself firmly, channeling her mother's no-nonsense tone. "There's got to be a logical explanation. You're a baker, not some nervous nellie in a mystery novel."

Ginger Snapped

Her green eyes swept the kitchen again, taking in details her anxious mind had missed before. That's when she spotted it – a faint scuff mark marring the usually spotless floor near the vintage display counter, its glass still bearing the original etched design from 1962.

Ginger's breath caught in her throat as she inched forward. The mark looked fresh, out of place in her meticulously maintained kitchen. As she rounded the corner of the counter, time seemed to slow, each heartbeat echoing in her ears.

"Oh my God!" The words escaped in a horrified gasp as her hand flew to her mouth.

There, sprawled on the Italian tiles she'd specially imported, lay Edith Fernwood. The town's most notorious gossip was unnaturally still, her impeccably styled silver curls fanned out like a macabre halo. The pastel cardigan she was never seen without was twisted awkwardly around her torso.

"Edith?" Ginger dropped to her knees beside the elderly woman, her baker's hands – usually so steady – shaking as she reached for a pulse. "Edith, can you hear me?"

No response. Edith's pale blue eyes, known for catching every detail of town gossip, stared blankly at the ceiling's original tin tiles.

"This can't be happening," Ginger whispered, panic rising in her chest like over-proofed dough. "Why are you even here? The bakery's been closed for hours!"

Her fingers fumbled with her phone, nearly dropping it twice before managing to dial 911. The screen's glow illuminated Edith's pallid features, making them seem even more ghostly.

"Focus," she scolded herself, hearing her father's voice in her head. "You're no good to anyone if you fall apart now."

As she waited for the call to connect, her gaze drifted to Edith's hand. There, clutched in fingers stiffened by death, was something that made Ginger's blood run cold – one of her signature gingerbread men, its traditional icing smile now seeming more like a sneer.

"911, what's your emergency?" The dispatcher's calm voice cut through Ginger's rising panic.

"This is Ginger Lawrence at Ginger Snaps Bakery on Main Street," she managed, forcing her voice to steady. "I need help. There's a woman unconscious in my bakery. She's not breathing, and I... I think she might be dead."

The wail of approaching sirens shattered the pre-dawn quiet before Ginger had even ended the call. Her heart leaped into her throat – she hadn't given them the address yet. Which meant...

Car doors slammed outside, followed by the heavy tread of boots on her freshly swept walkway. The bell above the door jangled discordantly as Detective Dan Griffith strode in, his presence filling the small space like thunder before a storm.

Dan's appearance had changed little since high school – still tall and broad-shouldered, with pepper-gray hair cropped close to his head. But his eyes, once warm with mischief during their shared chemistry classes, now held the sharp, assessing gaze of a man who'd seen too much.

"Ms. Lawrence," he said, voice gruff but not unkind. His eyes swept past her to where Edith lay. "We got an anonymous tip about a disturbance here."

Ginger's mind reeled. "A tip? But I just found her myself!"

Dan moved past her, crouching beside Edith's body with practiced efficiency. His frown deepened as he noticed the gingerbread man in her grip.

"One of yours?" he asked, though they both knew the answer. Every child and adult in Haversham Falls could recognize Ginger's distinctive gingerbread men, with their hand-piped details and secret blend of spices.

"Yes, but..." Ginger's voice faltered. "I didn't bake any yesterday. We were closed early for inventory."

Dan's head snapped up, eyes narrowing. "You're sure about that?"

"Positive. I haven't made them since Tuesday's batch, and those all sold out."

The detective stood, brushing off his knees. His next words fell heavy as lead in the quiet bakery: "Then we've got ourselves a problem, don't we?"

More officers filed in, their movements efficient and purposeful as they began transforming her beloved bakery into a crime scene. Yellow tape appeared across the doorway, and cameras flashed, documenting every detail of Edith's final moments.

"Tell me about your relationship with Mrs. Fernwood," Dan said, pulling out a small notebook.

Ginger Snapped

Ginger wrapped her arms around herself, suddenly cold despite the warming ovens. "We weren't close. She came in most mornings for coffee and a scone. Always complained the prices were higher than when my grandmother ran the place."

"Any recent disputes?"

"Nothing unusual. Just her regular comments about how things were better in the old days." Ginger's voice caught. "She was a pain sometimes, but she didn't deserve... this."

Dan's expression softened slightly. "No one deserves this, Ginger. But I need to ask – where were you between 9 PM and midnight last night?"

The use of her first name, a reminder of their shared history, made the question sting even more. "Here. Alone. Working on a new recipe for the Winter Festival."

"Can anyone verify that?"

"No," she admitted, frustration building. "But check the ovens – they're still warm from testing batches."

Dan circled her slowly, his shoes leaving scuff marks on her pristine floor. "Any reason Mrs. Fernwood would come here after hours?"

"None," Ginger insisted, her chef's whites feeling suddenly too tight. "I locked up at eight. You can check the security footage from Hal's Hardware next door."

"Yet here she is," Dan's tone dripped skepticism, "with one of your signature cookies."

Before Ginger could respond, a shout came from the kitchen: "Detective! You need to see this!"

Dan strode away, leaving Ginger alone with her thoughts and the growing fear that her life's work – this bakery that represented three generations of Lawrence women – might crumble like an overbaked cookie.

The next few minutes stretched like pulled taffy until Dan emerged, holding a small evidence bag containing crumbs. His expression had shifted, the doubt replaced by something closer to professional curiosity.

"These fragments," he said, holding them up to the light, "they're not from your recipe."

"What?" Ginger leaned closer, her trained baker's eye assessing the texture. "But I thought—"

"Mass-produced. Different spice profile entirely." Dan's voice held a note of respect. "Not your handiwork at all."

Relief flooded through Ginger, sweet as vanilla. "I told you. I'd never use my baking to harm anyone. It goes against everything my grandmother taught me."

Dan nodded, tucking the evidence away. "I believe you. But someone wanted us to think otherwise. The question is – who?"

As the investigation team packed up their equipment, Ginger surveyed her beloved bakery. Morning sunlight now streamed through the front windows, catching the dust motes disturbed by the police activity. The space felt different now, tainted by death and suspicion.

"We'll get to the bottom of this," Dan assured her, pausing at the door. "In the meantime, try to keep this quiet. Last thing we need is panic about poisoned baked goods spreading through town."

Ginger almost laughed at that. In Haversham Falls, keeping anything quiet was like trying to prevent dough from rising – virtually impossible.

As the last officer left, Ginger's mind was already racing. She knew every baker within fifty miles, every supplier, every brand of commercial gingerbread. If anyone could trace those store-bought crumbs, it was her.

"Sorry, Dan," she murmured to the empty shop, "but I can't just sit and wait. My bakery's reputation is at stake."

She glanced at the spot where Edith had lain, now marked only by forensic powder. "And you might have been a gossip, Edith Fernwood, but you deserve justice. Even if I have to bake it up myself."

Chapter

Ginger's hands trembled as she stared at the chaos enveloping her beloved bakery. Police tape crisscrossed the doorway, and officers swarmed around, dusting for fingerprints and bagging evidence.

"This can't be happening," she whispered, her voice barely audible over the din.

Detective Dan Griffith approached, his face grim. "Ms. Lawrence, I need to ask you a few more questions about your whereabouts last night."

Ginger's heart raced. "I already told you, I was here late baking for today's rush."

"Can anyone corroborate that?"

She shook her head, red curls bouncing. "I was alone."

Dan's eyes narrowed. "That's convenient."

"It's the truth!" Ginger's voice cracked. The scent of cinnamon and vanilla that usually comforted her now felt cloying, suffocating.

As the detective turned away, Ginger's gaze swept over the empty tables. The usual morning crowd was conspicuously absent. A lone customer hurried past the window, averting their eyes.

Ginger's shoulders slumped. "They all think I did it," she murmured.

The bell above the door jingled, and Ginger's heart leapt. But it was just another officer, not a customer.

She clenched her fists, flour-dusted nails digging into her palms. "I have to fix this. Somehow."

The weight of suspicion pressed down on her, heavier than any batch of dough she'd ever kneaded. But as she looked around at her life's work - the gleaming display cases, the worn butcher block counters - determination sparked within her.

Ginger straightened her apron. "I didn't kill Edith," she said firmly. "And I'll prove it."

Ginger's green eyes flashed with resolve. She strode to the front door, flipped the "Open" sign to "Closed," and locked it with a decisive click.

"Alright, Ging," she muttered to herself. "Time to channel your inner Nancy Drew."

She marched behind the counter, grabbed a notepad and pen, then paused. "Wait, what would Nancy do first?"

Ginger paced the length of the bakery, her footsteps echoing in the unnatural quiet. "Suspects. I need a list of suspects."

She scribbled furiously, flour-dusted fingers smudging the paper. "Who'd want Edith dead? Think, think!"

Her pen tapped an erratic rhythm on the counter. "The bridge club. They were always gossiping about something."

Ginger's brow furrowed. "And that new guy in town. What was his name? Tom? Tim?"

She shook her head, red curls bouncing. "Focus, Ginger. What about motives?"

Her gaze landed on a tray of gingerbread men, their icing smiles now seeming oddly sinister. "Money? Revenge? A secret Edith knew?"

Ginger's eyes widened. "The church fundraiser! Edith was in charge of the donations."

She scrawled another note, muttering, "Follow the money. That's what they always say in the movies, right?"

Pausing, Ginger surveyed her handiwork. The notepad was a mess of names, arrows, and question marks. "It's a start," she sighed. "But how do I prove any of this?"

Ginger's fingers trembled as she dialed the first number on her list. The phone rang three times before a gruff voice answered.

"Mrs. Benson? It's Ginger Lawrence from the bakery. I was hoping—"

"We don't want any cookies, dear." The line went dead.

Ginger stared at the phone, her cheeks flushing. "Well, that was rude."

She tried again, this time reaching Tom Peterson, the new guy in town.

"Mr. Peterson, I'm calling about Edith Fernwood. Did you—"

"Sorry, can't help you. Goodbye."

Click.

Ginger's jaw clenched. "What is wrong with everyone?"

She slammed the phone down, her green eyes blazing. "Fine. If they won't talk on the phone, I'll go to them."

Grabbing her coat, she marched out the door. The cool autumn air hit her face as she strode down Main Street.

Detective Dan Griffith appeared from around the corner, his blue eyes narrowing as he spotted her.

"Ms. Lawrence, what are you up to?"

Ginger lifted her chin. "Clearing my name, Detective. Since you won't."

Dan's expression hardened. "Leave the investigating to the professionals. You're only making yourself look more suspicious."

"I didn't kill Edith!"

"Then stop acting like you have something to hide." He turned away, dismissing her.

Ginger watched him go, her fists clenching at her sides. "I'll prove it," she whispered. "I'll prove I'm innocent if it's the last thing I do."

The bell above Ginger Snaps' door jingled as Ginger stepped back into her empty bakery. The silence engulfed her, a stark reminder of how quickly her life had unraveled. She sank into a chair, the weight of accusation pressing down on her shoulders.

"What am I doing?" Ginger whispered, burying her face in her hands. Her fingers trembled against her skin. "I'm a baker, not a detective. How can I possibly solve this?"

The clock ticked steadily, each second another reminder of her dwindling time. Ginger lifted her head, her green eyes glistening with unshed tears.

"But if I don't, who will?" She took a deep breath, squaring her shoulders. "Come on, Ging. You can do this."

Determination flickered in her gaze as she stood, striding purposefully to the back office. Ginger yanked open a drawer, pulling out a stack of old newspapers.

"Okay, Edith. Let's see what secrets you were hiding."

She spread the clippings across her desk, scanning headlines and photos. Her finger traced over an image of a younger Edith, standing proudly in front of the town hall.

"Town Gossip Uncovers Scandal," Ginger read aloud. "Huh. Looks like you've been stirring up trouble for years, Edith."

She grabbed a notepad, jotting down names and dates. As she worked, connections began to form, a web of relationships and old grudges taking shape.

"Oh!" Ginger's eyes widened as she spotted a familiar face in another photo. "I didn't know you two knew each other. This changes everything."

Her pen flew across the page, ideas and theories spilling out. For the first time since Edith's death, a spark of hope ignited in Ginger's chest.

"I'm coming for you," she murmured, determination etched in every freckle. "Whoever you are, I'll find you. And I'll clear my name."

Ginger's brow furrowed as she stared at the web of connections she'd drawn. "This doesn't make sense," she muttered, tapping her pen against the desk. "If Edith knew about the scandal, why didn't she expose it years ago?"

She shuffled through the clippings, frustration mounting. "Come on, there has to be something I'm missing."

Her fingers trembled slightly as she reached for another stack of papers. "Deep breaths, Ging. You can figure this out."

Ginger's eyes flicked between two conflicting articles. "Wait, how could Edith be at the town fair and meeting with the mayor at the same time?" She groaned, rubbing her temples. "This doesn't add up."

She stood abruptly, pacing the small office. "Think, Ginger. What would connect all these people?"

Her gaze fell on a faded photograph tucked beneath a pile of notes. Ginger's eyes widened as she snatched it up, heart racing.

"No way," she breathed, studying the image intently. "That's... that's the old Haversham mansion. Before the fire."

Her mind whirled, connections snapping into place. "The scandal, the secrecy, the conflicting stories... it all leads back to that night."

Ginger Snapped

"This is it. The key to everything." Ginger clutched the photo, a mix of excitement and trepidation coursing through her. "Now I just need to figure out what really happened at that mansion."

Ginger's heart raced as she grabbed her coat, the photograph clutched tightly in her hand. She rushed out of the bakery, the bell jingling wildly behind her.

"Mrs. Pendleton!" Ginger called, spotting her elderly neighbor sweeping her porch. "Have you seen Old Man Jenkins today?"

The woman squinted. "Saw him headed to that creaky old house of his 'bout an hour ago. Why?"

"Just need to ask him something. Thanks!" Ginger jogged down the street, her red hair bouncing with each step.

Her mind whirled as she approached Jenkins' dilapidated Victorian. If anyone knew about the mansion fire, it'd be him. He'd lived in Haversham Falls longer than anyone.

Ginger hesitated at the bottom of the porch steps. What if she was wrong? What if this lead went nowhere?

"No," she muttered, squaring her shoulders. "I have to try."

She climbed the stairs, wincing at each creak. Her hand trembled slightly as she raised it to knock.

"Well, here goes nothing," Ginger whispered, taking a deep breath.

Her knuckles hovered inches from the weathered door. What secrets lay behind it? What truths about that night at the mansion? And most importantly - would they finally clear her name?

Ginger steeled herself and knocked firmly, three sharp raps echoing in the still afternoon air.

Chapter

The kitchen timer chimed insistently as Ginger's fingers drummed against the worn marble countertop, her freckled face pinched with worry. The therapeutic scent of vanilla and almond wafted through the air – she'd stress-baked three batches of biscotti while trying to make sense of Edith's death. Cara methodically arranged the cooling cookies on vintage wire racks, the familiar routine providing a semblance of normalcy in their upended world.

"We need to talk to Mary, Neil, and Nelly," Ginger said, brushing flour from her cherished grandmother's apron – the one with hand-embroidered gingerbread men dancing along the hem. "They might know something about Edith that could help clear my name."

Cara looked up from her task, warm brown eyes resolute beneath wisps of escaped hair. She'd been stress-baking alongside Ginger since dawn, and a dusting of powdered sugar highlighted her dark curls like early snow. "Agreed. Where should we start?"

"Mary's café," Ginger decided, untying her apron and hanging it on the vintage copper hook by the bread station. "She knew Edith best – they shared morning coffee for twenty years." She paused, remembering the countless times she'd seen the two women huddled over steaming mugs, trading whispered conversations. "Ready for some detective work?"

Cara's lips quirked as she slid the last biscotti into place. "As I'll ever be. Let's go, Sherlock. Though shouldn't we call you Baker Street instead?"

Ginger Snapped

The autumn air nipped at their cheeks as they hurried down Main Street. The historic storefronts of Haversham Falls stood like sentinels, their brick facades witnessing a century of small-town secrets. Mary's Café occupied the corner spot where the town's first tea room had opened in 1902, and the original stained glass transom still cast rainbow patterns across the weathered hardwood floors.

The brass bell above the door chimed a welcome as they entered, releasing a wave of cinnamon and coffee aromas that wrapped around them like a warm embrace. Mary looked up from behind the vintage marble counter, where she was arranging her signature cranberry-orange scones on grandmother's cut-crystal cake stands.

"Ginger, Cara!" Mary's smile crinkled the corners of her eyes, though concern shadowed her gaze. "What brings you two in today? Surely not my scones – can't compete with your baking."

Ginger swallowed hard, the weight of her mission suddenly heavy. "We need to talk, Mary. About Edith."

Mary's hands stilled on the scone she was placing. She gestured to an empty booth tucked into the bay window, its cushions recently reupholstered in cheerful red-and-white gingham. "Have a seat, dears. I'll bring some tea. Something soothing – my special chamomile-lavender blend."

As Mary bustled away, Cara slid into the booth, her petite frame dwarfed by the plush cushions. "This won't be easy," she murmured, arranging sugar packets with nervous precision.

"But it's necessary," Ginger agreed, watching Mary steep their tea in her prized Brown Betty teapot, the one she claimed made every brew taste better.

Mary approached bearing a tray laden with steaming mugs and a plate of fresh-baked madeleines – her way of offering comfort through cuisine, a language all three women understood well. She set them down with practiced grace, the china clinking softly.

"Now," Mary said, settling across from them, "what's this about Edith? Terrible business, just terrible. Never thought I'd see such darkness touch our little town."

Ginger wrapped her hands around the warm ceramic, drawing strength from its steady heat. "We're trying to understand what happened. Did Edith have any enemies? Anyone who might have wanted to... hurt her?"

Mary's eyes widened, and she reached instinctively for a madeleine, crumbling it nervously between her fingers. "You can't possibly think..."

"We don't know what to think," Cara interjected softly, her voice as smooth as whipped cream. "That's why we're asking. You knew her better than anyone."

Mary's gaze darted between them, taking in their earnest expressions. She sighed heavily, dusting madeleine crumbs from her fingers. "Edith was... complicated. Like a temperamental soufflé – difficult to perfect but worth the effort. We were friends, but she could be..."

"Difficult?" Ginger prompted, remembering Edith's sharp comments about her "overpriced" gingerbread.

"She had strong opinions about everything – how I arranged my display case, why I should use loose tea instead of bags, whose pie should have won the harvest festival." Mary's fingers twisted her apron, a habit as old as her café. "But I never thought anyone would want her dead. This isn't that kind of town."

Cara reached across the table, squeezing Mary's hand. "We're just trying to understand. Any information could help clear Ginger's name."

Mary nodded slowly, her expression troubled. "I'll tell you what I know. But promise me you'll be careful. This town has secrets deeper than my grandmother's lasagna recipe, and some folks won't like them being dug up."

The bell above Neil's Hardware jangled discordantly as they entered, so different from the melodious chimes of their bakery and café. The scent of sawdust and metal struck their senses – a sharp contrast to the sweet aromas they'd left behind at Mary's.

Neil Bates looked up from where he was restocking shelf brackets, his weathered face creasing into a frown that had earned him the nickname "Thundercloud" among local children. "What can I do for you ladies? Need some new baking sheets?"

Ginger stepped forward, summoning the courage that helped her face down health inspectors and wedding cake emergencies. "We'd like to talk about Edith."

Neil's eyes narrowed beneath his bushy brows. His fingers tightened around the bracket in his hand. "What about her?"

"We're trying to understand what happened," Cara interjected, her voice as smooth as perfectly tempered chocolate. "To make sense of it all."

Neil grunted, setting down the bracket with deliberate care. "Tragic business, that. Like a perfectly good cake gone wrong – can't fix it, can't serve it, just have to deal with it."

Ginger's fingers twitched nervously, wanting to reach for her apron pocket where she usually kept her lucky wooden spoon. "Did you know her well?"

"Well as anyone, I suppose." Neil's gaze was sharp as a new paring knife. "Why're you asking?"

"We're just trying to piece things together," Ginger said, forcing a smile as sweet as her signature frosting.

Neil's jaw clenched like overdone pastry. "Listen here. I've known Edith since she tried to return a perfectly good hammer because it 'looked too used.' She was pickier than a food critic at a church potluck, but she was one of us. Don't go stirring up trouble like it's cake batter."

Their final stop was Nelly's Mystical Emporium, where the bell's tinkle mixed with the soft chiming of crystal wind chimes. The thick scent of jasmine incense wrapped around them, so different from the honest aromas of vanilla and butter they were used to.

Nelly glided towards them, her silver hair adorned with crystals that caught the light like sugar crystals on fresh-baked cookies. "Ah, the seeker and her loyal companion. The spirits whispered you'd come, like yeast sensing warm water."

Ginger suppressed an eye roll, remembering her grandmother's advice about catching more flies with honey than vinegar. "Nelly, we need to talk about Edith."

"The veil between worlds is thin today, like phyllo dough ready for baklava." Nelly gestured to a table adorned with crystals and tarot cards.

As they settled into their seats, Cara leaned forward, her voice gentle as folding whipped cream into mousse. "Did you and Edith have any... disagreements?"

Nelly's eyes sparkled like candied violets. "Edith was a stubborn oak in a forest of willows. We clashed like oil and water, but it was all part of life's recipe."

"Can you be more specific?" Ginger pressed, trying to keep the conversation from floating away like an untethered meringue.

"She disapproved of my methods. Called them 'hocus-pocus nonsense' while drinking my prosperity tea." Nelly's smile turned wistful. "But beneath her crusty exterior, Edith harbored deep-seated fears, like secrets hidden in a family cookbook."

As they left the shop, stepping back into the crisp autumn air, Cara turned to Ginger. "Well, that was..."

"About as clear as cloudy consommé," Ginger sighed. "But maybe useful. Edith was hiding something."

"But what?" Cara's brow furrowed like a poorly crimped pie crust. "And from whom?"

Ginger's mind whirled like egg whites in a stand mixer. "I don't know. But I'm starting to think Edith's death wasn't just about my gingerbread men. There's something else baking in this kitchen."

They walked back toward Ginger Snaps in thoughtful silence, the afternoon sun casting long shadows across Main Street. The comforting scent of baking bread from Alessandro's Italian restaurant mingled with the sharp autumn air, reminding them that life in Haversham Falls continued its familiar rhythms, even as they uncovered its hidden recipes for disaster.

"You know what this means," Cara said as they approached the bakery's familiar green awning.

Ginger nodded, her expression determined as she pulled her grandmother's recipe book from her apron pocket. "Time to do what we do best – gather the ingredients, follow the recipe, and solve this mystery one step at a time."

The bell above their door chimed a welcome as they returned to their culinary sanctuary. The afternoon sun streamed through the front windows, catching the display case just right and making the sugar-dusted pastries sparkle like freshly fallen snow.

"Let's review what we know," Cara said, pulling out her notebook – the same one she used for recipe testing, now repurposed for detective work. She settled onto a baker's stool, its worn wooden seat polished smooth by generations of Lawrence family bakers.

Ginger began pulling ingredients from the shelves, her hands moving automatically to gather what she needed for her grandmother's famous snickerdoodles. Baking always helped her think. "Mary mentioned Edith was agitated about 'setting things right.'"

"And Neil practically warned us off," Cara added, making notes in her precise handwriting. "Like a soufflé about to collapse."

"Then there's Nelly's cryptic comments about secrets." Ginger measured flour with practiced precision, the soft puffs of white dust catching the sunlight. "Everyone seems to be hiding something, like the secret ingredient in a prize-winning recipe."

The mixing bowl chimed softly against the marble countertop as Ginger began creaming butter and sugar. The familiar rhythm of baking soothed her nerves, even as her mind raced through possibilities.

"Don't forget what Detective Griffith said about the crumbs," Cara pointed out, absently catching a stray cinnamon stick that rolled toward the counter's edge. "Store-bought gingerbread, but made to look like yours."

Ginger's hands stilled over the bowl. "That's what's been bothering me. Why go to the trouble? Why not just use one of my actual cookies?"

The bell above the door chimed again, and both women looked up to see Alessandro Romano, owner of the Italian restaurant down the street. His usually cheerful face was creased with worry.

"Ginger, cara mia," he said, his accent thickening with emotion. "I heard about what happened. Terrible, terrible thing."

"Thanks, Al," Ginger smiled weakly. "How's Teresa doing with her wedding cake plans?"

Alessandro's expression darkened like an overdone crust. "That's partly why I'm here. There's something you should know. The night before... before Edith... I saw her arguing with someone outside my restaurant."

Ginger and Cara exchanged glances. "Did you hear what they were saying?" Cara asked, pen poised over her notebook.

"No, no, but..." Alessandro twisted his hands in his apron. "Edith seemed very upset. She kept pointing at a paper she was holding. And the other person – they grabbed it from her and stormed off."

"Could you see who it was?" Ginger asked, her heart beating faster than whipped cream in a stand mixer.

Alessandro shook his head regretfully. "It was too dark. But they were wearing a dark coat with a hood. Very mysterious, like something from a movie."

After Alessandro left, promising to let them know if he remembered anything else, Ginger turned to Cara. "A paper Edith was holding... something that made her upset enough to confront someone about it."

"And the next day she turns up..." Cara let the sentence hang like a cake testing toothpick.

The timer dinged, making them both jump. Ginger pulled the snickerdoodles from the oven, their sweet cinnamon aroma filling the kitchen. As she transferred them to a cooling rack, her eye caught the framed photo of her grandmother that hung beside the vintage spice rack.

"You know what Gran would say," Ginger mused, studying the familiar smiling face. "'The secret to any recipe is knowing not just what goes in, but what's been left out.'"

Cara's eyes lit up like perfectly caramelized sugar. "So maybe we need to look at what everyone's not saying."

"Exactly." Ginger reached for her phone. "And I think I know where to start. Remember how protective Neil was about Edith? There's got to be more to that story."

Just then, Ginger's phone buzzed with a text from Detective Griffith: "Need to talk. More evidence found. Come to station ASAP."

Ginger showed the message to Cara, her stomach knotting like badly worked dough. "What do you think? Another ingredient in our mystery mix?"

"Only one way to find out," Cara said, standing and brushing cinnamon sugar from her apron. "Though I have to say, for a small town baker, you're getting awfully good at this sleuthing business."

Ginger managed a small smile as she pulled her grandmother's recipe book from the shelf – the one with case notes now tucked between pages of cookie recipes. "Well, baking and detective work aren't so different. Both require precise measurements, careful observation, and..."

"The ability to handle things getting hot?" Cara suggested with a raised eyebrow.

"Something like that." Ginger locked the display case and flipped the "Back in 15 Minutes" sign on the door. As they stepped out into the crisp autumn air, she couldn't shake the feeling that they were about to uncover something bigger than a batch of store-bought gingerbread.

The late afternoon sun cast long shadows down Main Street as they walked toward the police station, their footsteps crunching through fallen leaves that smelled of autumn spices. The truth about Edith's death was out there somewhere, waiting to be uncovered like a long-lost family recipe. And Ginger was determined to find it, one careful ingredient at a time.

Chapter ★

The scent of cinnamon and vanilla wrapped around Ginger and Cara like a warm embrace as they huddled together at the corner table of Ginger Snaps Bakery. The vintage Edison bulbs overhead cast a gentle glow across the weathered maple table – the same one where Ginger's grandmother had rolled out her first batch of gingerbread men in 1962. Their heads were bent close over scattered papers, voices hushed despite the empty shop.

A batch of cardamom shortbread cooled on the nearby rack, its spicy-sweet aroma mingling with the ever-present notes of butter and sugar that perfumed the air. Ginger had stress-baked three batches since dawn, each one more perfect than the last. Baking had always been her way of thinking through problems, just as her grandmother had taught her.

"I can't believe what we've uncovered," Ginger whispered, her green eyes wide with the thrill of discovery. She tapped a flour-dusted finger on the notepad between them, leaving a powdery fingerprint beside Edith's carefully documented dates. "Look at these connections. Edith wasn't just being nosy – she was methodically digging into everyone's past."

Cara leaned in closer, her brow furrowed in concentration. The silver charm bracelet she always wore – a gift from Ginger on their tenth friendship anniversary – clinked softly against the table's edge. "But why? What was she hoping to find in all these old records?"

"I'm not sure yet, but..." Ginger bit her lip, mind racing like whipped cream in a stand mixer. The pieces were there, scattered like ingredients before a complex recipe. She just had to figure out how they fit together. "See how these dates line up? The baking competition in '85, the health inspection scandal in '92, the mysterious fire at the old mill in '97 – it's like she was tracking something specific."

"You're right." Cara's soft voice held a note of awe as she traced the timeline with her finger. "I never would have noticed that pattern. It's like... every seven years or so, something happened that changed the town's dynamics."

Ginger sat back in her chair, hands automatically fidgeting with the embroidered gingerbread men that danced along her apron strings – her mother's handiwork from years ago. Her heart raced with the thrill of discovery, tempered by a twinge of unease that felt like underproofed dough. What secrets had Edith unearthed in her investigation? And more importantly, had those secrets gotten her killed?

"We need to keep digging," she said firmly, channeling her grandmother's no-nonsense tone. "There's more here, I can feel it in my bones – like knowing when a cake is done without checking the timer."

Cara nodded, her quiet strength as dependable as a well-calibrated oven. She pulled out her notebook – the same one where she recorded recipe variations and customer preferences. Now it held something far more dangerous than baking notes. "Where do we start?"

"I think..." Ginger hesitated, then squared her shoulders like she was preparing to face a health inspector. "I think we need to talk to Mary Ashton. Really talk to her."

Cara's eyebrows shot up like over-proofed bread. "The café owner? Why her specifically?"

"Just a hunch." Ginger's fingers drummed on the table in the same rhythm she used for kneading bread. "But look at Edith's notes – they keep circling back to Mary. The '85 baking competition, the disputed property line in '92, the argument at the town council meeting last spring. There's something there, Cara. I'm sure of it."

As Ginger spoke, her excitement grew like a perfect soufflé. This was it – the breakthrough they needed. She could feel it in her bones, as sure as she knew when a batch of cookies was perfectly baked.

"Let's go now," she said, pushing back from the table with sudden energy. "Before I lose my nerve. Before anyone else can get to her first."

Cara caught her arm gently, like handling delicate spun sugar. "Are you sure about this, Ging? We don't want to upset anyone unnecessarily. Mary's been a fixture in this town longer than we've been alive."

Ginger paused, considering her friend's words. Cara was right to be cautious – she always had been the voice of reason in their friendship, the one who made sure recipes were tested thoroughly before going on the menu.

"I have to know, Cara," she said softly, her voice barely louder than the gentle hum of the refrigerator cases. "For the bakery. For the town. For me. Someone tried to frame me for murder using my own signature recipe. I can't just let that sit, like a fallen cake in the window."

Understanding filled Cara's warm brown eyes. "Alright then. Let's go solve this mystery. But first..." She gestured to Ginger's flour-covered apron and hands.

"Right." Ginger managed a small smile. "Probably shouldn't interrogate a potential suspect looking like I've been wrestling with a bag of flour."

While Ginger cleaned up, Cara gathered their evidence, carefully organizing the papers into categories: newspaper clippings, handwritten notes, and photographs. Each piece was a potential ingredient in the recipe of truth they were trying to assemble.

"Look at this," Ginger murmured, pausing in washing her hands to tap a faded photograph with one damp finger. "Edith with Mary Ashton, must be from the late '70s or early '80s."

Cara leaned in, studying the image. "They look... tense. Not exactly friendly."

"Exactly. And here—" Ginger shuffled through Edith's handwritten notes with now-clean hands. "She mentioned a 'betrayal' involving Mary. Something about 'stolen dreams' and 'false promises.'"

"What kind of betrayal are we talking about?"

Ginger's green eyes flashed like copper pots catching sunlight. "That's what we need to find out. And look at this – it gets more interesting."

Cara picked up a yellowed newspaper clipping, its edges crisp despite its age. Someone had preserved it carefully. "'Local rivalry heats up at annual bake-off,'" she read aloud. "'Edith Fernwood claims foul play after surprising upset. Long-time favorite defeated by newcomer Mary Ashton's innovative take on traditional recipes.'"

Ginger Snapped

The implications hung in the air like the scent of burning sugar. Ginger's mind raced through the possibilities, each one more troubling than the last. "So Edith thought Mary cheated in the competition? But why dig this up now, after all these years?"

"Maybe it wasn't just about the competition," Cara suggested, her voice thoughtful. "What if there was something bigger? Something that's been simmering all these years, like a reduction sauce?"

Ginger's fingers drummed on the counter again, a nervous habit she'd developed during her first baking competition. "You think Edith was blackmailing Mary? That she found something worth killing over?"

"It's possible." Cara bit her lip, considering. "But we need more proof. These are serious accusations, Ging. We can't half-bake this theory."

They exchanged a loaded glance, the weight of their discoveries settling between them like a heavy dusting of powdered sugar. The sunny afternoon beyond the bakery windows seemed at odds with the darkness of their conversation.

Ginger began to pace the length of the bakery, her practical shoes squeaking slightly on the well-worn floors. Her grandmother had paced these same boards, working through her own problems over the years. "We need to dig deeper, Cara. There's more to this story – I can feel it."

Cara's brow furrowed with concern. "Ging, we should be careful. We're bakers, not detectives. This isn't like testing a new recipe where the worst that can happen is a failed batch."

"But I'm the one under suspicion!" Ginger's voice rose like bread in a hot oven. "I can't just sit back and let my bakery suffer. Three generations of Lawrence women built this place. I won't be the one to let it crumble."

"I understand, but—"

"No buts." Ginger's eyes blazed with determination. "We need to confront Mary, get her side of the story. Force her hand."

Cara stood, placing a gentle hand on Ginger's arm like tempering chocolate – careful, steady pressure. "That's too risky. What if she panics?"

"Then we'll know she's hiding something." Ginger shrugged off Cara's touch, too agitated to be soothed.

"Or she could call the police." Cara's tone sharpened like a well-honed knife. "Think about it, Ging. Detective Griffith already suspects you. How would it look if you started interrogating other townspeople?"

Ginger's shoulders tensed. "So what, we do nothing? Let the real killer walk free while my reputation goes up in flames?"

"We gather more evidence. Quietly. Like proving a recipe before it goes on the menu."

The bell above Mary's café door jingled as Ginger and Cara stepped inside, its cheerful tone at odds with their grim purpose. The cozy space, usually as warm and inviting as freshly baked bread, felt charged with an undercurrent of tension that made Ginger's skin prickle.

Her eyes darted around, cataloging details with the same precision she used for checking ingredient measurements. The café looked normal – too normal, perhaps. Every table was perfectly set, each napkin folded with military precision, as if Mary had been stress-cleaning.

The aroma of fresh coffee and baked goods hung in the air, a familiar comfort that did nothing to ease the knot in Ginger's stomach. She spotted Mary behind the counter, methodically wiping down the espresso machine with the focus of someone avoiding their thoughts.

"Ready?" Ginger whispered to Cara, who gave a slight nod.

They approached the counter, their footsteps echoing in the nearly empty café. Mary looked up at their approach, her usual warm smile in place, though it didn't quite reach her eyes.

"Ginger, Cara!" Mary's voice held its usual cheer, but there was an undertone of something else – tension, perhaps, or fear. "What a lovely surprise. Can I get you some tea? I just got in a new lavender blend."

Ginger swallowed hard, gathering her courage like ingredients for a complex recipe. "Actually, Mary, we need to talk to you about something important."

Mary's smile faltered slightly, like a soufflé losing its rise. "Oh? What about?"

"It's about Edith," Cara interjected, her voice low and steady.

Mary's hand stilled on the cleaning cloth. "Edith? What about her?"

Ginger leaned in, lowering her voice to avoid being overheard by the elderly couple in the corner sharing a scone. "We know you two had a... complicated relationship. We need to understand why."

Mary's eyes widened, and for a moment, Ginger caught a glimpse of real fear in them. "I'm not sure what you mean."

"Please, Mary," Ginger pressed, her heart pounding like a rolling pin on tough pastry. "We're trying to piece together what happened. Did Edith ever threaten you? Or your café?"

Mary's gaze flicked between them, her sunny demeanor cracking like overdone shortbread. "Girls, I don't think—"

"We're not accusing you," Cara added quickly, her voice smooth as ganache. "We just need to know the truth."

Tension crackled in the air like sugar under a torch as Mary hesitated, her fingers twisting the cloth into knots. Finally, her shoulders slumped, the cheerful façade crumbling completely.

"Not here," she said quietly, glancing at her remaining customers. "Follow me."

She led them through the swinging kitchen doors into a small office that smelled of old receipts and coffee grounds. Every surface was meticulously organized – recipe files in alphabetical order, invoices sorted by date, old photographs arranged carefully on the walls.

Mary sank into a worn leather chair behind her desk, suddenly looking every one of her sixty-plus years. "You girls might want to sit down for this. It's... it's quite a story."

Ginger and Cara exchanged glances as they settled into the visitor chairs. This was it – the moment of truth they'd been seeking, like opening the oven to check a perfectly baked cake.

"Edith and I weren't always enemies," Mary began, her voice barely above a whisper. "We were best friends once. More than that – we were going to be business partners."

The revelation hit Ginger like a fallen soufflé. "What?"

"It was 1985. We had dreams of opening the best bakery-café Haversham Falls had ever seen. We even had a name picked out – Sweet Dreams." Mary's eyes grew distant, lost in memories. "But we had different visions. I wanted something cozy, traditional. Edith... she wanted to experiment, push boundaries. She thought we could compete with the big city bakeries."

Cara leaned forward, her reporter's notebook forgotten in her lap. "What happened?"

"We fought. Badly. Said things we couldn't take back." Mary's fingers drummed nervously on her desk. "Then came the baking competition. We both entered, each trying to prove our vision was better. I won with my classic scones, but Edith... she never believed the judging was fair."

"Did she have reason to doubt it?" Ginger asked carefully.

Mary's eyes filled with tears. "That's the worst part. She did. I... I had help with my recipe. From someone who shouldn't have been involved."

The truth hung in the air like the scent of burnt sugar – impossible to ignore, impossible to hide.

"Who?" Ginger pressed gently.

Mary's voice dropped even lower. "Judge Harrison. He was... we were... involved. He gave me inside information about what the judges were looking for. Edith found out recently. She had proof."

Ginger's mind raced. "Is that why she was in your café the night before she died?"

Mary's head snapped up. "How did you know about that?"

"We didn't," Cara said softly. "Until now."

Mary's face crumpled. "She threatened to expose everything. Not just the competition – other things too. Things that would ruin me. But I swear, I didn't kill her. I was here all night, doing inventory. You can check the security cameras!"

Ginger and Cara exchanged looks. They believed her – Mary might have cheated at a baking competition, but murder seemed beyond her capabilities. But if Mary wasn't the killer, who was? And what other secrets had Edith uncovered?

As they left the café, stepping into the crisp autumn air, Ginger's mind whirled with possibilities. "So Edith was blackmailing people with their past secrets. But why now? After all these years?"

Cara shook her head, her expression troubled. "And why use your gingerbread men to do it? Someone wanted to frame you specifically, Ging. We need to figure out why."

Chapter 3

The bell above the bakery door jingled its familiar melody as Ginger stepped inside, the comforting aroma of vanilla and cinnamon wrapping around her like her grandmother's well-worn apron. Detective Dan Griffith followed close behind, his solid presence as reassuring as a perfectly preheated oven. The morning light streamed through the vintage stained-glass transom, casting rainbow patterns across the polished maple countertops.

Ginger's heart quickened, and not just from anticipation of sharing her discoveries. There was something about Dan that made her feel both unsettled and grounded, like the moment before opening the oven door to check a soufflé. "Thanks for coming so early, Detective. I hope we can make some progress today."

"That's the plan." Dan's blue eyes, sharp as a master chef's knife, scanned the room with professional precision. The morning sun caught the silver at his temples, reminding Ginger that he'd been serving Haversham Falls since before she'd taken over the bakery. "Any new developments?"

"Actually, yes." Ginger smoothed her apron – the one with dancing gingerbread men that her mother had embroidered – more out of habit than necessity. "I've been working on something I'd like to show you."

She led him to the back office, her fingers brushing against the cool brass of the doorknob. The small room, usually reserved for reviewing recipes and planning menus, had been transformed into an investigation headquarters. Ginger flicked on the light, illuminating the evidence board she'd meticulously crafted on the wall where her culinary certificates usually hung.

Dan's eyebrows rose appreciatively, and Ginger felt a flutter of pride in her chest. "Impressive work, Ms. Lawrence. You've got quite an eye for detail."

"Just like baking," she said, then felt her cheeks warm at the comparison. "I've been connecting the dots as best I can."

She watched as Dan studied the board, his sharp gaze taking in every detail – the newspaper clippings, the timeline, the web of relationships she'd mapped out with different colored strings. His proximity sent a shiver down her spine that had nothing to do with the early morning chill.

"What's your take on Neil Bates?" Dan pointed to the hardware store owner's photo, worn at the edges from years behind his counter's glass display case.

Ginger frowned thoughtfully. "He and Edith had a falling out over a business deal years ago. Something about a joint venture that went sour. Could be motive."

"Agreed. And Mary Ashton?" His finger moved to the café owner's smiling face.

"She was close to Edith once, but something about her story doesn't add up – like a recipe with a missing ingredient." Ginger stepped closer to the board, accidentally brushing against Dan's arm. The contact sent sparks through her that she tried desperately to ignore.

Dan nodded, a ghost of a smile playing on his lips. "You've got good instincts. Better than some detectives I know."

Their eyes met, and for a moment, the tension between them crackled like static electricity. Ginger could smell his aftershave – subtle and spicy, like her favorite chai blend.

She cleared her throat, forcing herself to focus on the case. "So, what do you think? Any theories?"

Dan's gaze returned to the board, but Ginger noticed how his body remained angled toward hers. "It's clear there's more to this case than meets the eye. We need to dig deeper into these relationships, find out what everyone's hiding."

"I was thinking the same thing." Ginger's fingers fidgeted with her apron strings. "Maybe we could interview them together? Two sets of eyes might catch what one would miss."

Dan considered her suggestion, his expression thoughtful. "That could work. You know these people, their habits. And you've proven yourself observant."

Ginger's heart leapt at his acceptance, though she tried to keep her voice steady. "Great. Where should we start?"

"Let's begin with Neil. His motive seems the strongest, and the hardware store opens early."

As they made their way through the bakery, Ginger caught a flash of red near where Edith's body had been found. "Dan, look at this." She crouched down, pointing to a small smudge on the Italian tile floor.

Dan knelt beside her, his shoulder brushing hers. "Red icing?"

"Not just any red icing." Ginger leaned closer, her nose almost touching the floor as she inhaled. "This is my signature raspberry buttercream. I only use it for special orders, and I haven't made any in weeks."

Their eyes met, a spark of understanding passing between them. The discovery hung in the air like the scent of burning sugar – impossible to ignore, impossible to hide.

"This could be significant," Dan said, his voice low and intimate in the quiet bakery. "Someone either had access to your recipes or..."

"Or went to a lot of trouble to make it look like they did," Ginger finished. She was acutely aware of their proximity, of how Dan's cologne mixed with the bakery's sweet aromas.

The hardware store's bell clanged harshly as they entered – so different from the melodious chime of Ginger's bakery. Neil looked up from behind the counter, his weathered face set in its usual scowl.

"What do you want?" His gruff tone matched the store's utilitarian atmosphere.

Dan stepped forward, badge out. "Mr. Bates, we'd like to ask you about Edith Fernwood."

Neil's scowl deepened, like a cake left too long in the oven. "What about her?"

Ginger spoke up, her voice steady despite her racing heart. "We understand you two had some... business troubles in the past."

"Ancient history," Neil growled, but Ginger noticed how his calloused hands clenched on the counter.

"Maybe," Dan said, "but history has a way of repeating itself. Did you have any recent conflicts with Edith?"

As Neil spoke, Ginger's gaze wandered the cluttered space, landing on a framed photograph partially hidden behind a display of measuring tapes. She blinked in surprise.

"Is that you and Edith?" she asked, interrupting Neil's defensive monologue.

Neil glanced at the photo, his gruff demeanor faltering like a soufflé in a slammed oven. "Yeah. Long time ago."

Dan leaned in, interested. "You two look... close."

Neil's weathered face softened slightly, years seeming to fall away. "We were. Once upon a time."

The revelation hung in the air like spun sugar, delicate and unexpected. Ginger stepped closer, her curiosity piqued. "What happened?"

Neil sighed, running a hand through his graying hair. "Business deal. Went south. Edith... she wasn't always the easiest person to work with."

"Care to elaborate?" Dan pressed, his detective's instincts sharp as a well-honed knife.

Neil's eyes hardened again. "It was supposed to be a partnership. Expand the hardware store, add a bakery section. But Edith... she wanted control. Pushed me out."

Before Ginger could respond, Dan's phone buzzed. He glanced at the screen, his eyebrows shooting up like perfectly peaked meringue.

"We've got a tip," he said quietly. "Someone saw Nelly Grimes near the bakery the morning of the murder."

The investigation led them to Nelly's Mystical Emporium, where the soft tinkling of crystal wind chimes greeted them instead of a traditional bell. The scent of incense and herbs enveloped them – sage, lavender, and something exotic Ginger couldn't quite identify.

Nelly emerged from behind a beaded curtain, her silver hair adorned with tiny crystals that caught the light. "Ah, the baker and the detective. The cards told me you would come."

Ginger's eyes were drawn to a glinting object around Nelly's neck – a small gingerbread man charm that looked suspiciously familiar.

Dan cleared his throat. "We have some questions about your whereabouts on the morning of Edith's murder."

As the investigation deepened, so did the connection between Ginger and Dan. Every shared glance, every accidental touch, every moment of unspoken understanding added another layer to their relationship, like the delicate sheets of a perfect mille-feuille.

Their final confrontation with Mary in her café felt like a recipe gone terribly wrong. The warm, homey space turned cold and hostile as Mary's façade crumbled, revealing the darkness beneath her sweet exterior.

"I just wanted to talk to her," Mary sobbed, her carefully maintained appearance dissolving like sugar in hot tea. "But she laughed at me. Said she'd ruin everything I'd built."

The arrest was quick and efficient, but it left a bitter taste in everyone's mouth. Outside the café, Dan's hand found Ginger's, offering warmth and comfort in the autumn chill.

"You okay?" he asked softly.

Ginger shook her head, watching as Mary was led away in handcuffs. "I never thought... Mary, of all people. It's like finding out your favorite recipe book was filled with poison all along."

Dan's thumb traced gentle circles on her palm. "You can't always see the darkness in people. Even in a town as sweet as this one."

Later that evening, they sat across from each other at Alessandro's Italian restaurant, candlelight dancing between them like sugar crystals catching the sun. The case was closed, but something else was just beginning to rise.

"To solving the mystery," Dan raised his wine glass, his blue eyes twinkling in the soft light.

"To new partnerships," Ginger responded, feeling a warmth that had nothing to do with the excellent Chianti.

As they shared tiramisu – Alessandro's secret recipe – Ginger realized that sometimes the sweetest things in life come after the most bitter moments. Like the perfect balance of flavors in a well-crafted dessert, she and Dan had found their own unique blend of chemistry.

The mystery was solved, but their story was just beginning to proof, like a promising batch of dough set aside to rise.

Chapter 1

The morning sun streamed through Ginger Snaps Bakery's windows, catching the display case just right and making the sugar-dusted pastries sparkle like freshly fallen snow. Ginger stood behind the counter, methodically piping rosettes onto a batch of cupcakes, trying to lose herself in the familiar rhythm. But even the therapeutic nature of baking couldn't quite settle her mind after yesterday's events.

Mary's arrest had shaken the entire town. The café across the street remained dark, its windows like hollow eyes staring accusingly at Ginger's cheerfully lit bakery. The regular morning customers who usually split their time between both establishments now huddled in Ginger's shop, their whispered conversations rising and falling like steam from fresh-baked bread.

The bell above the door chimed, and Ginger looked up to see Cara rushing in, her cheeks flushed from the crisp autumn air. "Have you seen this morning's paper?"

Before Ginger could answer, Cara slapped the Haversham Herald onto the counter, narrowly missing a tray of cooling snickerdoodles. The headline made Ginger's stomach lurch: "Local Baker Helps Crack Murder Case: More Secrets Coming to Light?"

"They're calling you the 'Pastry Detective,'" Cara said, sliding onto a baker's stool. "But that's not even the interesting part. Look at page three."

Ginger wiped her hands on her apron – her lucky one with the dancing gingerbread men – and flipped to the indicated page. Her eyes widened as she read: "Sources suggest victim Edith Fernwood may have been involved in multiple blackmail schemes. Police investigating connection to cold cases."

"Cold cases?" Ginger's voice dropped to a whisper. "What kind of cold cases?"

The bell chimed again, and Detective Dan Griffith strode in, looking more rumpled than usual. His blue eyes met Ginger's, sending that now-familiar flutter through her chest.

"Just the baker I wanted to see," he said, managing a tired smile. "Got a minute?"

Cara shot Ginger a knowing look as she gathered her things. "I'll handle the front counter. You two talk."

In the small office that had served as their investigation headquarters, Dan ran a hand through his silver-streaked hair. "Mary's talking. A lot. Turns out Edith's blackmail scheme went back decades."

Ginger perched on the edge of her desk, still cluttered with their case notes. "What kind of secrets could be worth killing over in a town like this?"

"That's what we need to find out." Dan pulled out his notebook. "Mary mentioned something about a file – said Edith kept detailed records of everyone's secrets. But we haven't found it."

"And you think it might be here? In my bakery?"

Dan nodded. "Edith was here the night she died. If she had the file with her..."

"It could still be hidden somewhere," Ginger finished, her mind already racing through possibilities. "We should start with the vintage cabinets. They're original to the building, full of hidden compartments."

As they searched, Ginger was acutely aware of Dan's presence – his subtle cologne mixing with the bakery's sweet aromas, the way his shoulder brushed hers as they examined tight spaces. The investigation might be officially closed, but something told her their partnership was just beginning.

"Wait," Dan said suddenly, his hand stilling on the back panel of a lower cabinet. "Feel this."

Ginger knelt beside him, her fingers finding the slight irregularity in the wood. With a soft click, a hidden panel swung open, revealing a thick manila envelope.

"Jackpot," Dan breathed.

Together, they spread the contents across Ginger's desk. Letters, photographs, newspaper clippings – decades of secrets laid bare. Ginger's heart pounded as she began to read.

"Oh my god," she gasped. "Dan, look at this. The fire at the old mill in '97? It wasn't an accident. And the health inspection scandal at Le Petit Café? That was staged too."

"Edith was collecting evidence," Dan mused, sorting through the papers. "But why? What was her endgame?"

Before Ginger could respond, a sharp crash came from the front of the bakery, followed by Cara's startled cry. They rushed out to find Neil Bates standing in a puddle of broken china, his weathered face pale.

"Is it true?" he demanded, waving the morning's paper. "About Edith's files? About the cold cases?"

Dan stepped forward, one hand moving toward his badge. "Mr. Bates, I'm going to need you to calm down."

But Neil's eyes were fixed on Ginger. "You don't understand. If those files get out... people's lives will be ruined. Good people, who made mistakes years ago."

"Like you?" Ginger asked softly, remembering the old photograph in his shop.

Neil's shoulders sagged like a fallen soufflé. "We were young. Stupid. The mill fire... it wasn't supposed to happen like that."

"Neil Bates," Dan's voice was firm but gentle, "I think you'd better come down to the station with me."

As Dan led Neil away, Ginger's mind whirled like egg whites in a stand mixer. How many more secrets were hidden in Edith's files? How many more lives would be affected?

Cara appeared at her elbow, armed with a dustpan and brush. "You okay?"

"I'm not sure," Ginger admitted, watching through the window as Dan helped Neil into his patrol car. "I thought solving Edith's murder would be the end of it. But it feels more like the beginning."

"Whatever comes next," Cara said firmly, "we'll handle it together. Like we always do."

The rest of the day passed in a blur of customers and questions. Everyone wanted to know about Mary's arrest, about Neil's outburst, about the rumors of more secrets to come. Ginger stuck to her grandmother's advice: keep your hands busy and your mouth shut. She baked three batches of comfort cookies, two dozen emergency scones, and enough bread to feed half the town.

As the sun began to set, casting long shadows across the bakery floor, the bell chimed one last time. Dan stood in the doorway, looking exhausted but somehow lighter.

"Neil confessed," he said without preamble. "To the mill fire, at least. Said it was an insurance scheme gone wrong. Edith found out somehow, kept the evidence all these years."

Ginger began gathering ingredients for her grandmother's famous hot chocolate – the kind reserved for serious conversations. "How many more confessions do you think are coming?"

"Hard to say." Dan accepted the steaming mug she offered, their fingers brushing in the exchange. "But I could use your help going through those files. Your knowledge of the town, the people... it could be invaluable."

"Are you asking me to be your official consultant, Detective Griffith?" Ginger tried for a light tone, though her heart was racing faster than her industrial mixer.

Dan's tired face broke into a genuine smile. "I'm asking if you'd be willing to be my partner in solving some very cold cases. Over dinner, perhaps?"

The warmth that spread through Ginger's chest had nothing to do with the hot chocolate. "I think I could be persuaded. Assuming there's good food involved."

"Alessandro's? Tomorrow night?" Dan's eyes held more than just professional interest. "We can discuss the case files over his famous tiramisu."

"It's a date," Ginger said, then felt her cheeks flush. "I mean, a meeting. A professional dinner meeting."

Dan's smile widened. "Right. Professional. Though maybe we could discuss something other than murder over dessert?"

As he left, Ginger caught Cara's knowing grin from across the bakery. Her friend mimed writing in the air – probably already planning to update their case notebook with this new development.

Ginger turned back to her kitchen, her safe haven in the midst of all this chaos. Tomorrow would bring more secrets, more revelations, more complications. But for now, she had cookies to bake, a date to plan for, and the satisfying knowledge that justice, like the perfect recipe, sometimes took time to get just right.

She pulled out her grandmother's recipe book, its pages worn and butter-stained from decades of use. Between the familiar instructions for breads and pastries, she began a new entry: "How to Solve a Murder and Find Love in a Small Town - A Recipe in Progress."

The bell above the door tinkled one last time as Cara left for the night, calling over her shoulder, "Don't forget to wear that new blue dress tomorrow!"

Ginger laughed, already mentally planning her outfit while measuring ingredients for tomorrow's bakes. In Haversham Falls, it seemed, justice was best served with a side of romance and a sprinkle of sugar.

Chapter 4

The aroma of freshly baked cinnamon rolls wafted through Ginger Snaps bakery, their sweet perfume mingling with the tension hanging in the air like sugar crystals in saturated syrup. Ginger Lawrence wiped her flour-dusted hands on her grandmother's lucky apron, the embroidered gingerbread men dancing along its hem seeming to mock her worried expression.

"Neil Bates has to be involved somehow," Ginger said, pacing behind the vintage maple counter that had witnessed three generations of Lawrence women's triumphs and troubles. "He's the only one with a clear motive, and Mary's confession mentioned him specifically."

Detective Dan Griffith leaned against the display case, his piercing blue eyes following Ginger's movements like a master chef watching a soufflé rise. The morning light streaming through the bakery's stained-glass transom window caught the silver at his temples, reminding Ginger that despite their growing closeness, he was still very much a professional.

"We can't jump to conclusions without evidence," he cautioned, though his tone held more warmth than warning. "That's a recipe for disaster."

Cara Noonan perched on a nearby baker's stool, her petite frame dwarfed by the bustling kitchen but her presence as essential as vanilla in a classic recipe. "But the blackmail angle, Dan. That has to count for something. Mary admitted Edith was threatening multiple people."

Ginger's mind raced faster than her industrial mixer on high speed. Could Neil really have murdered Edith over her meddling? The gruff hardware store owner had always seemed harmless, if a bit prickly – like an overproofed bread dough that just needed gentle handling.

"We need concrete proof," Ginger declared, slamming her palm on the counter. A puff of flour rose into the air like a ghostly warning. "Something that will stick better than a failed meringue."

Dan raised an eyebrow, the ghost of a smile playing at his lips. "And how do you propose we get that without compromising the official investigation?"

Cara's eyes lit up like perfectly caramelized sugar. "What if we visited Neil's store? A bit of reconnaissance under the guise of needing supplies?"

"Brilliant!" Ginger nodded eagerly. "The annual health inspection is coming up. We could say we need new safety equipment."

"Hold on," Dan interjected, his voice stern but his eyes betraying concern. "You can't just go snooping around. That's police work."

Ginger fixed him with a determined stare, channeling every ounce of her grandmother's famous backbone. "With all due respect, Detective, your job isn't getting done fast enough. My reputation – my family's legacy – is on the line. And after what we found in Edith's files..."

Her voice trailed off, remembering the damning documents they'd discovered hidden in her bakery's vintage cabinetry. The old mill fire, the health inspection scandal, decades of secrets that had simmered like a reduction sauce, growing more potent with time.

Cara placed a gentle hand on Ginger's arm, steady as a perfectly calibrated oven. "We'll be careful, Dan. Promise. No half-baked schemes."

Dan sighed, running a hand through his hair in a gesture Ginger had come to find endearing. "Fine. But you follow my lead on this. And we do it together."

Ginger's heart skipped like a jumping souffle, though whether from the thrill of investigation or Dan's protective tone, she couldn't quite say.

The bell above Neil's Hardware chimed discordantly as they entered – so different from the melodious tinkle of Ginger's bakery bell.

Ginger Snapped

The scent of sawdust and metal assaulted their senses, a sharp contrast to the sweet aromas they'd left behind.

"Act natural," Ginger whispered, though her heart was beating faster than whipped cream in her stand mixer. "Like we're just here for supplies."

Cara nodded, picking up a nearby paintbrush with convincing interest. "You know, we really should think about repainting the bakery's trim. That sage green is looking a bit tired."

Neil's gruff voice carried from the back room like a timer going off. "Be with you in a minute!"

Ginger's eyes darted around, taking in every detail with the same precision she used for decorating wedding cakes. A cluttered workbench caught her attention – specifically, a familiar floral scent that seemed out of place among the industrial aromas.

"Is that..." she whispered to Cara, "Edith's perfume?"

Before Cara could respond, heavy footsteps approached like rolling thunder. Neil emerged, wiping his hands on a rag that had seen better days. His eyes narrowed when he spotted them, suspicious as a health inspector faced with questionable refrigeration.

"What brings you two here?" His tone was sharper than a new bread knife.

Ginger summoned her best customer service smile – the one she reserved for particularly difficult wedding clients. "Just browsing. The health inspector mentioned we might need some updates to our safety equipment."

Neil's gaze bore into them like a laser thermometer. "Safety equipment? Funny timing, considering all that's happened."

The tension in the air thickened like overworked pastry dough. Ginger opened her mouth to respond when a sound from the back room caught her attention – a metallic clang followed by what sounded suspiciously like cursing.

Neil's face darkened like an overbaked cookie. "Store's closed. You need to leave. Now."

But Ginger's instincts were screaming louder than a timer left unattended. That voice in the back room... she knew that voice.

Before Neil could stop her, she darted past him, ignoring his shout of protest. She burst through the stockroom door just in time to see a figure disappearing through the back exit. But not before she caught a glimpse of something that made her blood run cold – a familiar charm bracelet, identical to the one found clutched in Edith's hand the morning of her death.

"Ginger!" Dan's voice rang out behind her, followed by the sound of running footsteps. He must have been watching from outside, just as they'd planned.

She turned to face him, her mind whirling like beaten egg whites. "Dan, you're not going to believe who I just saw."

But before she could explain, a crash from the front of the store cut through the air like a dropped baking sheet. They rushed back to find Neil gone and Cara standing amid a scatter of fallen tools, her face pale as uncooked pastry.

"He ran," she said, pointing toward the front door. "But not before I saw what he was trying to hide."

She held up a small leather-bound notebook, its pages stuffed with what looked like receipts and photographs. "I think we just found Edith's missing blackmail evidence."

Dan pulled out his phone, already dialing for backup. But Ginger barely heard him. Her eyes were fixed on a photograph that had fallen from the notebook – a decades-old image of Neil, Mary, and another familiar face she'd seen just moments ago, all standing in front of the old mill. The date stamp read one day before the mysterious fire.

The pieces were falling into place like ingredients in a complex recipe. But this time, the final product promised to be more bitter than sweet.

Chapter

The shattered glass crunched under Ginger's feet like sugar crystals in a failed meringue as she approached Nelly's vandalized shop. Tarot cards and crystals littered the sidewalk, their mystic promises scattered like ingredients in an upended pantry. An acrid smell of smoke lingered in the air, reminding Ginger uncomfortably of burnt gingerbread.

Detective Dan Griffith's jaw clenched as he surveyed the damage, his trained eyes cataloging each detail with the precision of a master baker measuring spices. "Third incident this week. First Mary's café gets broken into, then Neil's store, now this."

"This is getting out of hand." Ginger's voice cracked like a poorly tempered chocolate. She bent to pick up a fallen crystal, its once-smooth surface now scratched and clouded. "First the threats, then Mary's confession about the blackmail, and now this?"

Cara squeezed her friend's arm, steady as a well-calibrated oven. "We won't let it escalate further."

But Ginger's instincts, honed by years of knowing exactly when to pull a cake from the oven, told her they were missing something crucial. The vandalism felt calculated, like a recipe designed to distract from the main course.

"I need answers about Edith's murder. Now." Her tone hardened like cooling caramel. "Before things get worse."

Dan's piercing blue eyes met hers, concern mixing with professional detachment. "We're doing everything we can. The lab results from the gingerbread crumbs—"

"It's not enough." Ginger gestured at the destruction around them, her baker's hands moving expressively. "Whoever did this isn't going to stop. Look at the pattern – they're targeting people connected to Edith's blackmail scheme."

A chill ran down her spine as she pictured her beloved bakery in similar ruin. The thought of her grandmother's vintage copper bowls shattered, her mother's hand-embroidered aprons torn... The image made her blood run cold as frozen butter.

The trio stepped into Nelly's shop, where flickering candles cast strange shadows across walls hung with crystals and dream catchers. The overwhelming scent of sage and jasmine wrapped around them like an overly complex spice blend.

Nelly emerged from behind a beaded curtain, her silver hair wild as whipped egg whites and her eyes wide behind crystal-studded glasses. "Oh my, what a surprise! The cards told me visitors would come, but they didn't say who."

Ginger's gaze swept the shop, taking in details others might miss – the slight disarray that seemed too artful, the way certain crystals had been carefully arranged amid the chaos. Like a display case made to look casually elegant, it felt staged.

"Nelly," Dan began, his detective's tone gentle but firm, "we need to talk about Edith. And about this." He gestured to the vandalism.

"Ah, yes." Nelly sank into a velvet armchair that had somehow escaped damage. "The universe works in mysterious ways, doesn't it?"

"Let's focus on more earthly matters," Ginger pressed, noting how Nelly's fingers twisted nervously in her lap. "Like why someone would target your shop right after we found those letters in Neil's store."

Nelly's serene expression flickered like a candle in wind. "Letters? What letters would those be?"

"The ones about the old mill fire," Cara supplied softly. "The ones that mentioned you by name."

The air in the shop seemed to thicken like over-whipped cream. Nelly's face paled beneath her ethereal makeup.

"That was so long ago," she whispered. "Ancient history, like a recipe yellowed with age."

"But history has a way of rising to the surface," Dan said, "like secrets in a small town."

Ginger Snapped

Ginger moved closer to an ornate cabinet that had caught her eye – its dark wood gleaming oddly in the candlelight. Something about its brass fittings struck her as familiar.

"This is beautiful," she commented, running a finger along its edge. "Antique?"

"Oh, that old thing?" Nelly's voice held a note of panic. "Just a family piece. Nothing special."

But Ginger had already spotted what made it unique – the maker's mark matched the one on the mysterious cufflink they'd found near Edith's body. A discovery she carefully kept from her expression.

"Interesting craftsmanship," she mused. "Reminds me of some of the vintage pieces in my bakery. Speaking of which, Nelly, I never got to thank you for those special crystals you recommended for my kitchen. What were they called again?"

It was a trap, carefully baited. They'd never discussed crystals for the bakery. Nelly's response would be telling.

"Oh, the... rose quartz?" Nelly ventured, her usual confidence wavering like a soufflé in a slammed oven.

Ginger shared a quick glance with Dan. Another lie to add to the growing pile.

Cara, meanwhile, had drifted to a shelf of old books, her gentle demeanor masking sharp observation skills. "These grimoires look ancient. Family heirlooms?"

"Yes, passed down through generations." Nelly's reply came too quickly.

"Like this?" Cara carefully lifted a leather-bound volume, revealing a receipt dated just last month from "Mystical Manuscripts & More."

The tension in the room could have been cut with a pastry knife. Nelly's carefully constructed façade began to crack like overdone shortbread.

"I can explain," she began, but a sudden crash from outside made them all jump.

Glass tinkled onto the pavement, followed by the screech of tires. Dan rushed to the window while Ginger's mind raced ahead like a runaway mixer.

The vandalism, the staged chaos, Nelly's lies – it was all connected, but how? Like a complex recipe, each ingredient had its purpose. They just needed to figure out the right order.

Her phone buzzed in her pocket. Unknown number.

The message made her blood freeze: "Stop digging into Nelly's past. Or you'll be joining Edith sooner than you think."

But below it was something else – a photo. Grainy but clear enough to recognize three figures standing before the old mill: Nelly, considerably younger but unmistakable; Mary, looking nervous; and Neil, holding something that glinted in the sunlight.

A crystal pendant identical to the one found clutched in Edith's dead hand.

The pieces were there, like ingredients laid out on a counter. Now they just had to figure out how they came together – before someone decided Ginger needed to be removed from the recipe entirely.

Chapter 6

Ginger's fingers brushed against a dusty cardboard box as she reached for the vanilla extract on the top shelf of the storage room. The familiar scent of baking spices surrounded her – cinnamon, nutmeg, and her grandmother's secret blend that had made Ginger Snaps famous. But something felt off, like a recipe with an ingredient slightly out of balance.

She frowned at the unmarked box, tucked carefully behind jars of molasses and bags of specialty flour. It didn't belong among her meticulously organized supplies. "What's this doing here?"

Setting aside her search for vanilla, Ginger pulled the box down, sending a small cloud of dust dancing in the early morning light that filtered through the high storage room window. The cardboard was worn soft at the corners, suggesting years of handling despite its hidden location.

Her heart quickened as she lifted the lid. Old photographs spilled out like ingredients from an overturned mixing bowl – her parents, looking impossibly young, standing outside the courthouse. Her mother's auburn hair, so like Ginger's own, caught the sunlight in the faded image. Her father's usually confident stance seemed uncertain, his arm protectively around his wife.

But it was the newspaper clippings that made her breath catch: "Local Couple Implicated in Fraud Scheme" screamed one headline. "Environmental Cover-Up Rocks Small Town" declared another. Legal documents covered in dense text completed the damning collection.

"No... it can't be." Ginger's hands trembled as she sifted through the papers, each new discovery adding another crack to her carefully constructed world. A letter in her mother's distinctive handwriting caught her eye: "We never meant for it to go this far..."

Her father's signature on what appeared to be a plea deal made her stomach lurch. The dates aligned perfectly with the old factory scandal – the same period Edith had been investigating before her death.

"They were involved. All this time..." Ginger's voice echoed in the small storage room, bouncing off shelves lined with the tools of her trade – rolling pins, cake pans, cookie cutters that had been passed down through generations of Lawrence women.

She grabbed another handful of papers, scanning frantically. Dates, names, amounts – the evidence of her parents' involvement in the scandal that had nearly torn Haversham Falls apart twenty years ago was irrefutable.

"How could they keep this from me?" Her fingers shook so badly she could barely hold the documents. The floor seemed to tilt beneath her feet, and Ginger sank down, surrounded by the physical proof of her parents' deceit.

The truth lay scattered around her like shattered china – impossible to ignore, impossible to make whole again. Her parents – the ones who'd taught her to bake, who'd supported her dreams of taking over the bakery, who'd instilled in her the importance of honesty and integrity – were at the center of the very scandal that now threatened to destroy everything.

Ginger's mind raced as she paced the cramped storage room, her footsteps echoing off shelves stacked with bags of flour and sugar. The familiar scents of vanilla and almond extract that usually brought comfort now seemed to mock her.

"I have to know why," she declared, her green eyes flashing with determination in the reflection of a metal mixing bowl.

She burst out of the storage room, nearly colliding with a rack of rolling pins. The hallway stretched before her like an endless path, leading to the front of the bakery where she could hear her parents' voices mixed with the morning crowd's cheerful chatter.

The swinging door yielded to her push, the hinges protesting with a squeak that seemed to emphasize her agitation. The bell above jangled discordantly, startling the customers inside. The usual warm aroma of fresh-baked goods hung in the air, but to Ginger, it suddenly felt cloying.

"Mom, Dad, I need to talk to you." Her voice carried over the murmur of conversation, tight with barely contained emotion.

Marianne and Nate stood behind the counter, serving a tray of gingerbread men to Mrs. Henderson, whose weekly order hadn't changed in fifteen years. They looked up at Ginger's entrance, their warm smiles freezing as they caught sight of her face.

"Sweetheart, what's wrong?" Marianne asked, concern etching the lines around her eyes – lines Ginger had always attributed to years of laughter, but now wondered if they'd been carved by guilt.

The bakery fell silent as Ginger's hands gripped the edge of the maple counter – the same counter where she'd learned to roll dough, where her mother had taught her that precision and patience were the keys to perfect pastry. Now it felt like the only solid thing in a world that had suddenly turned fluid.

"Why didn't you tell me?" Her voice cracked, a mix of hurt and anger that seemed to echo off the vintage tin ceiling tiles. "All these years, you've been hiding this from me?"

The customers turned, eyes wide with the kind of curiosity that only small-town drama could inspire. Mrs. Henderson's gingerbread men lay forgotten on their decorated plate. Even Old Mr. Peterson, who'd been coming in for his morning scone since before Ginger was born, set down his coffee cup with a concerned clink.

Marianne's face paled, her hand fluttering to her throat where she wore the silver locket Nate had given her when they first opened the bakery. The same year, Ginger now realized, as the factory scandal.

"Ging, honey, let's take this to the back," Nate said, his usual calm demeanor strained like overworked dough.

"No." Ginger's voice rose, filling the space like bread in a hot oven. "I want answers. Right here, right now. The whole town deserves to know the truth."

Marianne and Nate exchanged worried glances, guilt shadowing their expressions like dark clouds before a storm. The same expressions Ginger had seen in the old courthouse photographs.

"Please, sweetie," Marianne pleaded, reaching for Ginger's hand across the counter dusted with powdered sugar. "This isn't the place-"

Ginger jerked away, her motion sending a shower of sugar into the air. "When were you planning to tell me? Or were you just hoping I'd never find out about your involvement in the factory scandal?"

A collective gasp rose from the customers. Mrs. Abernathy's jaw dropped, her half-eaten scone suspended midair like a pause in time.

Nate stepped forward, his voice low and urgent. "Ginger, we can explain. But not like this. Not here."

"Explain what?" Ginger demanded, her green eyes flashing like copper pots catching sunlight. "How you've been lying to me my entire life? How you covered up environmental violations that could have poisoned the whole town?"

The bakery fell silent, the air thick with tension and the lingering scent of cinnamon. Even the ancient wall clock seemed to tick more quietly, as if afraid to interrupt.

"I deserve the truth," Ginger insisted, her voice growing louder with each word. "All of it. The factory, the cover-up, everything. No more lies."

Marianne's eyes darted nervously around the bakery, taking in the audience of regular customers who'd become more like family over the years. "Ginger, please-"

"No." Ginger's voice quivered like a soufflé in a slammed oven. "I found the box. The photos, the documents..." She swallowed hard, fighting back tears. "How could you be part of something like that?"

Nate's shoulders slumped, his usual strong presence diminished like a fallen cake. "We never meant to hurt anyone. We thought we were protecting the town."

"But you didn't protect it, did you?" Ginger's laugh was bitter as over-steeped tea. "You helped cover up pollution that could have made people sick. That could still be making people sick."

The bell above the door jingled as a customer walked in, then quickly retreated, sensing the tension. The sound seemed to break something in Marianne.

"You're right," she said softly, her voice barely carrying over the hum of the refrigerated display case. "You deserve to know everything. But it's complicated, sweetheart. So complicated."

Ginger's hands clenched into fists, flour drifting from her knuckles like snow. "Then uncomplicate it. I'm not a child anymore. I can handle the truth."

Ginger Snapped

The silence stretched like pulled taffy, broken only by the gentle tick of the clock and the soft whir of the ceiling fans.

Finally, Nate spoke, his voice heavy with regret. "It started twenty-five years ago. The town was dying. The old mill had closed, shops were shuttering, and we were desperate to keep our new business afloat."

"The bakery?" Ginger asked, though she already knew the answer from the documents.

"And your father's carpentry shop," Marianne added softly. "We had just opened, had a new baby – you – and the factory promised to bring life back to Haversham Falls."

"We made a deal," Nate continued, his blue eyes clouded with memories. "With the factory owners. They would steer business our way, help keep us afloat, if we... helped them with certain paperwork."

Ginger's heart raced as the pieces fell into place. "The environmental reports. You falsified them."

Marianne nodded, tears spilling onto her flour-dusted cheeks. "We didn't understand the full implications at first. By the time we realized how serious the pollution was-"

"We were in too deep," Nate finished. "They had evidence of our involvement. They threatened to expose us, to take everything we'd built."

Ginger's anger began to waver, replaced by a confusing mix of emotions that swirled like marble in pound cake batter. "So you just... continued? Let them keep polluting?"

"No," Marianne said quickly. "We tried to find a way out. That's when we went to the authorities. Made a deal to expose the bigger players in exchange for immunity."

"But the damage was done," Nate added heavily. "The river had already been contaminated. People were getting sick, though it would be years before anyone made the connection."

Ginger's mind raced. "And Edith? Did she know about all this?"

Her parents exchanged a significant look. "Edith... she was investigating. Had been for years," Marianne admitted. "She believed there was more to the story than what came out in the official investigation."

"And was there?" Ginger pressed, remembering the threatening notes, the vandalism, Mary's confession about blackmail.

"Maybe," Nate said carefully. "But if there was, it died with Edith."

The implications of that statement hung in the air like smoke from a burned cake. Ginger's investigator's mind began connecting dots she hadn't seen before.

"This is why you've been so worried about my involvement in solving Edith's murder," she realized. "You knew she was investigating the factory scandal. You were afraid of what I might uncover."

Marianne reached across the counter again, and this time Ginger didn't pull away. "We were trying to protect you, sweetheart. But you're right – you deserve to know the truth. All of it."

"Then tell me," Ginger said, her voice stronger now. "Everything you know about Edith's investigation, about the factory, about who might have wanted to silence her. No more secrets."

Nate nodded solemnly. "No more secrets. But Ginger... some of what we know... it could be dangerous."

"I don't care," Ginger declared, squaring her shoulders. "Edith deserves justice, and this town deserves the truth. Whatever the cost."

As her parents began their story, Ginger noticed movement near the door. Detective Dan Griffith stood in the entrance, his expression unreadable as he took in the scene.

Their eyes met, and Ginger saw understanding dawn in his face. This wasn't just about Edith's murder anymore. This was about decades of secrets, lies, and corruption that had poisoned Haversham Falls like toxic waste in its river.

The truth might be bitter, but like the perfect balance of flavors in a complex recipe, it was necessary for healing to begin.

Dan moved through the bakery with quiet authority, his presence adding weight to the already heavy atmosphere. "Mrs. Lawrence, Mr. Lawrence, I think you'd better tell us everything you know about the factory scandal. It might be relevant to our current investigation."

Mrs. Abernathy leaned forward, her forgotten scone now completely cold. "The factory scandal? But that was twenty-five years ago! My Henry worked there, before the... troubles."

"The troubles that nobody talks about," Old Mr. Peterson added, his weathered hands wrapped around his coffee cup. "The mysterious illnesses, the fish dying in the river, the crops that wouldn't grow right."

Ginger Snapped

Nate's face grew grave. "It wasn't just environmental reports we helped cover up. The factory was disposing of something far worse than industrial waste. Something that Edith discovered just before..."

"Before she died," Ginger finished, her mind racing like an overlocked mixer. "That's what she meant in her diary about 'patterns repeating.' The same people involved in the factory scandal are connected to what's happening now."

Marianne's hands twisted her apron. "There were meetings, late at night at the old mill. The factory owners would come with briefcases full of documents – and cash. They paid off half the town to keep quiet."

"Including Mary's father," Nate added quietly. "He was the environmental safety inspector. And Neil's uncle owned the trucking company that transported the waste."

The pieces began falling into place like layers in a perfectly assembled mille-feuille. Ginger turned to Dan, her eyes wide with realization. "The vandalism, the threats, Mary's confession about blackmail – it's all connected to the factory scandal!"

"But why now?" Cara asked, having slipped into the bakery during the revelations. "Why would someone kill Edith after all these years?"

"Because she found proof," Marianne whispered, reaching beneath the counter to pull out another box, this one metal and locked. "She came to us last month, showed us these. We... we were too afraid to act on them then."

With trembling hands, she produced a key and opened the box. Inside lay photographs – crystal clear images of drums being buried behind the factory, their hazard symbols clearly visible. And more recent photos showing the same area, now developed into the new town park.

"The paradise garden project," Dan muttered, examining the photos. "They're building a children's playground right over..."

"A toxic waste dump," Nate finished grimly. "Edith figured it out. She traced the shell companies, followed the money. She could prove who was really behind it all."

"The same people who are now on the town council," Ginger realized, thinking of the recent development meetings she'd attended. "The ones pushing for the park project to begin immediately."

Mrs. Henderson stood suddenly, her face pale. "My granddaughter... she's been sick. The doctors can't figure out why. We just moved into the new houses near the old factory site..."

A murmur of concern rippled through the gathered crowd. More voices joined in, sharing stories of unexplained illnesses, mysterious odors, gardens that wouldn't grow.

"We have to stop them," Ginger declared, looking at her parents. "No more secrets, no more cover-ups. The truth comes out now."

Dan pulled out his phone. "I'm calling in the Environmental Protection Agency. And the state police. This is bigger than a small-town murder now."

"They'll try to stop us," Marianne warned, fear evident in her voice. "These people... they're powerful. Connected."

"Let them try," Ginger said firmly, squaring her shoulders. "We have something they don't – proof. And a whole town of witnesses ready to speak up."

Nate stepped around the counter to stand beside his daughter. "We'll tell everything we know. It's time to make things right."

The bell above the door chimed again, and Rebecca Fernwood – Edith's niece – burst in, clutching a manila envelope. "I found it! Aunt Edith's final evidence. The proof of who's really behind everything!"

But before she could say more, a shot rang out. The bakery window shattered, sending glass and terrified screams through the air like thrown ingredients.

"Get down!" Dan shouted, pulling Ginger behind the counter as another shot cracked through the morning quiet.

As they huddled together – family, friends, neighbors – Ginger realized that the recipe for justice would require more than just truth. It would need courage, solidarity, and the strength of an entire town ready to stand up against decades of corruption.

And somewhere out there, a killer was realizing that their carefully constructed plan was crumbling like overworked pastry.

Chapter

Ginger's hand trembled as she reached for the mixing bowl, her instincts screaming that something was wrong. The familiar kitchen of Ginger Snaps Bakery felt different, like a beloved recipe made with ingredients subtly out of balance. The usual comforting scents of vanilla and cinnamon seemed muted, overshadowed by an inexplicable sense of dread.

Her eyes darted around the space she knew as well as her own heartbeat, noticing small discrepancies that set her nerves on edge. The flour canister perched on the wrong shelf, its position just slightly off, like a cake that had settled unevenly. Her favorite spatula – the one with the hand-carved handle her father had made – lay in the sink instead of hanging from its designated hook, where it had lived for the past five years.

Ginger's heart quickened, its rhythm matching the steady tick of the vintage wall clock. "Hello?" she called out, her voice echoing off the copper pots hanging overhead. "Is someone here?"

Only silence answered, broken by the soft hum of the refrigerator cases. The morning light filtering through the windows cast strange shadows across the floor, making familiar shapes seem threatening.

She shook her head, flour dust dancing in her copper curls. "Get it together, Ging," she whispered, trying to calm her racing thoughts. "You're just paranoid after everything that's happened." The words sounded hollow even to her own ears.

But as she turned back to her work, a faint scraping sound echoed from the storage room – the same room where she'd found Edith's body just weeks ago. The sound was deliberate, like metal against wood.

Ginger froze, blood pounding in her ears like water in a copper pot about to boil over. The morning quiet suddenly felt oppressive, dangerous.

"Okay, deep breaths," she whispered, her grandmother's advice floating through her mind. "It's probably just a mouse. Or the wind." But mice didn't move spatulas, and the wind couldn't rearrange flour canisters.

Her fingers closed around the handle of a heavy rolling pin – the one she used for Danish pastry, its maple wood worn smooth from years of use. Not much of a weapon, but its familiar weight offered some comfort.

Ginger crept toward the storage room, each step carefully placed to avoid the creaky floorboard near the prep table. The early morning sun cast long shadows through the windows, making the usually cozy bakery feel like a stage set for something sinister.

Another scrape, louder this time, followed by what sounded like papers being shuffled.

She pressed her back against the wall beside the door, her baker's apron rustling softly. Her pulse raced faster than her industrial mixer on high speed. The rolling pin felt slick in her sweating palms.

"Who's there?" Ginger's voice shook despite her attempt at bravery. "I'm calling the police!"

No response came from beyond the door. Just that eerie silence that felt like the calm before a storm.

Ginger's hand hovered over the doorknob, its brass surface reflecting the morning light. Part of her screamed to run, to get out while she still could. But she had to know. Too many secrets had already been buried in this town, like bitter flavors masked by sweet frosting.

She took a deep breath, steadying herself like she would before opening a temperamental oven. In one fluid motion, she flung open the door.

Ginger's eyes widened in shock as she came face to face with Mayor Thompson, his hand clutching a kitchen knife that gleamed wickedly in the dim light. His usually jovial face, the one that smiled from campaign posters all over town, had transformed into something hard and cruel.

Ginger Snapped

"You!" she gasped, stumbling backward, her rolling pin raised defensively. "But... why? What are you doing here?"

Mayor Thompson's expression twisted into a sneer that would have looked more at home on a villain in a noir film than on the face of Haversham Falls' most prominent citizen. "You just couldn't leave well enough alone, could you, Miss Lawrence? Had to keep digging, like your friend Edith."

The mention of Edith's name sent a chill down Ginger's spine. Her grip tightened on the rolling pin as pieces of the puzzle began falling into place. "The factory scandal, the environmental cover-up, the development project – it was all you, wasn't it?"

"Clever girl," Thompson said, advancing slowly. "Just like your parents. They knew when to keep their mouths shut. Too bad you didn't inherit that trait."

Fear clawed at Ginger's throat like underproofed bread dough, but she lifted her chin defiantly. The Lawrence women had never backed down from a fight, and she wouldn't be the first. "Never. I know what you did. Mrs. Abernathy figured it out too, didn't she? That's why she had to die."

"Such spirit," Thompson chuckled darkly, the sound as bitter as burnt sugar. "It's almost a shame to snuff it out. But we can't have anyone connecting the dots between the old factory site and the recent... incidents."

Ginger's mind raced faster than a stand mixer on high speed. She needed to keep him talking, buy time. "Why her? What did Mrs. Abernathy discover?"

"Nosy old bat was digging into my finances, traced the shell companies I used to buy up the contaminated land. She had to go." Thompson's casual tone made the confession even more chilling. "Just like Edith, poking around where she didn't belong. One heart attack, one unfortunate fall – accidents happen all the time in a small town."

"You won't get away with this," Ginger declared, her voice steady despite her racing heart. Her eyes darted to the prep table, calculating distances and angles like measuring ingredients for a complex recipe.

Thompson's eyes narrowed, cold as frozen butter. "I already have, my dear. And you'll be next if you don't back off. We can do this the easy way – you leave town, take that pretty little bakery somewhere else. Or..." He let the threat hang in the air like smoke from a burned cake.

"I won't be bullied," Ginger spat, channeling her grandmother's famous backbone. "This town deserves the truth about what you've done."

"The truth?" He laughed bitterly. "The truth is, you're in way over your head, little baker girl. Just like your parents were, before they learned their lesson."

Ginger's gaze darted around the kitchen, assessing her options like reviewing ingredients before a complex bake. The back door was too far, but the prep table... Her fingers inched toward a large bag of flour.

"You're right about one thing," she said, inching sideways. "I am a baker."

In one fluid motion, she snatched up the flour bag and hurled it at Thompson's face. The bag burst on impact, engulfing him in a white cloud that would have been comical under different circumstances.

"Argh!" he sputtered, temporarily blinded by the impromptu smokescreen.

Ginger seized her chance. She grabbed a heavy copper baking sheet from the nearby rack and swung it with all her strength, connecting solidly with Thompson's knife hand. The blade clattered to the floor like a dropped measuring spoon.

"You little—" he growled, lunging for her through the settling flour dust.

Ginger ducked under his grasp and bolted for the front of the bakery, her practical shoes squeaking on the tile floor. Her fingers fumbled with the lock, adrenaline making her usually precise movements clumsy.

"Come back here!" Thompson's roar echoed through the bakery, accompanied by the crash of falling equipment.

The door finally gave way, and Ginger burst onto Main Street. The cool morning air stung her flushed cheeks as she sprinted past darkened storefronts, their windows reflecting her flight like silent witnesses.

"Help!" she screamed into the pre-dawn quiet, praying someone would hear. "Somebody help me!"

Heavy footsteps pounded behind her, each one driving her forward like a heartbeat marking time in a practiced recipe. Thompson was giving chase, his usual dignified mayoral persona completely stripped away.

"You can't run forever, Ginger!" he bellowed, his voice carrying the weight of decades of secrets and lies.

Ginger Snapped

She risked a glance back. The flour-covered mayor was gaining ground, his face contorted with a rage that transformed his familiar features into something monstrous.

Chapter 6

Ginger's pulse thundered as she and Cara edged deeper into the abandoned warehouse. The scent of rust and damp concrete clung to the air, each creak of the warped floorboards echoing like a gunshot. Shafts of moonlight struggled through grime-coated windows, casting long, sinister shadows.

"Are you sure this is the place?" Cara whispered, clutching her tote bag like a lifeline. Her dark eyes darted toward every flicker of movement.

Ginger nodded, red curls bouncing despite the tight knot of anxiety coiled in her chest. "The note said to look behind the third pillar on the left. It has to be here."

Her voice was steadier than she felt. Every instinct screamed at her to turn back, to abandon this foolhardy search, but she couldn't. Not after everything. She couldn't fail Cara—or Edith.

They crept forward, the silence pressing down on them like a weight. Ginger's fingers twitched with the phantom memory of her rolling pin. She'd left it at the bakery, convinced it would look suspicious. A choice she now bitterly regretted.

Cara stiffened as a rat scurried past, its claws scratching against metal. "I hate this place," she muttered, shaking off the moment. "It feels... wrong."

"It is," Ginger agreed, her voice low. "But we're close. I can feel it."

Ginger Snapped

The third pillar loomed ahead, an imposing monolith of cracked concrete. Ginger crouched, her hands grazing its rough surface, searching for something—anything—that would justify the risk.

"There has to be a hidden compartment or..." Her voice trailed off as her fingers snagged on an irregular groove. A loose brick. Her pulse quickened as she tugged it free, revealing a narrow cavity.

"Cara," Ginger hissed, motioning her over.

Inside was a crumpled piece of paper, stained and brittle. Ginger's hands trembled as she unfolded it. The faint, spidery handwriting sent a chill down her spine.

"What does it say?" Cara leaned in, her breath shallow.

Ginger scanned the note, her eyes widening with every word. "It's a confession... and a warning." Her voice wavered. "This wasn't just about Edith. Someone's trying to scare us away—"

A deafening crash shattered the silence. Both women spun around, their hearts leaping into their throats. Heavy footsteps reverberated through the warehouse.

"They know we're here," Ginger breathed. Her hands flew to her pockets, shoving the note inside. "Run!"

They bolted toward the exit, adrenaline surging through their veins. The echo of footsteps grew louder, closing the distance. Ginger risked a glance back, her breath hitching. A shadowy figure was gaining on them.

Cara stumbled, nearly falling. Ginger caught her arm, yanking her upright. "Don't stop!" she gasped.

The door loomed ahead, glowing like salvation. They burst into the open air, the sudden sunlight blinding. Ginger squinted, disoriented, as Cara pulled her toward the car.

"Keys! Hurry!" Cara shouted, diving into the passenger seat.

Ginger fumbled, the keys slipping from her trembling hands. Finally, the engine roared to life. She slammed the gear into reverse, tires squealing as they sped away. Relief flickered, but it was short-lived.

Behind them, the figure emerged, brandishing a glinting blade.

"Look out!" Cara screamed as the figure lunged, the knife embedding itself in the headrest beside her. Ginger swerved, throwing the attacker off balance.

"The flour!" Cara cried, fumbling with her tote.

Ginger understood. "Do it!"

Cara flung a cloud of flour into the figure's face, blinding them. Ginger hit the brakes, sending the assailant tumbling. But the victory was fleeting. The figure recovered quickly, lunging again.

"Cara, the cinnamon!"

Without hesitation, Cara hurled the spice into the attacker's eyes. They howled, clutching their face, giving the women precious seconds.

Ginger's relief turned to horror as the attacker rebounded, their blade slashing. Cara screamed, the knife grazing her arm before Ginger swung her rolling pin with all her strength. The wooden tool cracked against the attacker's head.

But the fight wasn't over. The assailant tackled Cara to the ground. Ginger's heart seized as Cara's head struck the pavement with a sickening thud.

"No!" Ginger's scream tore through the air as blood pooled beneath Cara's hair.

The attacker loomed over Cara's motionless body, blade poised to strike. Desperation burned in Ginger's chest. She couldn't lose her best friend. Not now, not ever.

"Get away from her!" Ginger roared, charging with a ferocity she didn't know she possessed.

The figure turned, slashing. Pain flared across Ginger's arm, but she didn't stop. Her fingers closed around the attacker's wrist, wrestling for control.

A screech of tires cut through the chaos. Ginger's head snapped up as an SUV barreled toward them.

"Mom! Dad!" she cried, her voice breaking.

The car skidded to a halt, and Marianne Lawrence leapt out, her silver hair wild in the wind. Nate followed, his broad frame radiating resolve.

"Marianne, help Cara!" Ginger pleaded, collapsing to her knees.

Marianne didn't hesitate, rushing to Cara's side. Nate grabbed Ginger, his hands steadying her trembling shoulders. "You're safe now," he murmured.

The wail of sirens grew louder, and Detective Dan Griffith appeared, his weapon drawn. His piercing blue eyes swept the scene, taking in the blood, the chaos, the trembling young woman before him.

"Secure the area," he barked to the officers. Then, to Ginger, his voice softened. "What happened here?"

Ginger Snapped

Ginger recounted the harrowing events, her voice breaking. Dan listened intently, his jaw tight.

When the paramedics loaded Cara into the ambulance, Ginger felt her knees buckle. Marianne caught her, holding her close. "It's not your fault," she whispered.

"But it is," Ginger choked out. "I dragged her into this."

"Stop," Nate said firmly. "You saved her life."

Detective Griffith approached, his gaze steady. "Ginger, what you did was brave."

"Brave?" Her voice cracked. "I almost got her killed."

"You faced a killer and lived to tell the tale," Dan said. "That takes guts. And it's not over. We'll catch them. Together."

Ginger straightened, fire reigniting in her chest. For Cara. For Edith. She would find justice.

No matter what it took.

The ambulance pulled away, its sirens wailing, and Ginger stood frozen, watching the taillights disappear. Every nerve in her body screamed at her to follow Cara to the hospital, but Dan's hand on her shoulder grounded her.

"Ginger, stay with me," he said, his tone gentle but commanding. "You're in shock. Let's take this step by step."

She swallowed hard, nodding. Her mind was a whirlwind of guilt, fear, and simmering rage. "I need to help her. I need to do something."

"You're doing it now," Dan assured her. "Every detail you give me is a step closer to finding the bastard who did this."

Marianne wrapped a blanket around Ginger's shoulders. "Sweetheart, you've done enough for tonight. Let the police handle it from here."

Ginger shook her head fiercely. "No. This isn't over. Not until I know who's behind this."

Nate's hand rested heavily on her shoulder. "We're not saying to stop, Ginger. But you need to regroup. Going in guns blazing won't help Cara—or you."

Dan gave a short nod, his gaze locking onto Ginger's. "Your dad's right. You're smart, but you need to be strategic. Whoever this is, they're dangerous. Recklessness could cost you your life."

The weight of his words settled over her, sobering and chilling. She hated the helplessness gnawing at her. "Fine. But as soon as Cara's stable, I'm back in this."

Dan's lips quirked in the faintest of smiles. "Wouldn't expect anything less."

Later that night, Ginger sat at the kitchen table, a cup of untouched tea cooling in her hands. The events of the day played on a loop in her mind: Cara's scream, the flash of the blade, the attacker's menacing glare. She closed her eyes, the image of Cara's blood pooling on the pavement seared into her memory.

"Ginger," Marianne's voice broke through her thoughts. She slid into the chair across from her daughter, her expression etched with concern. "Talk to me, sweetheart."

Ginger stared at the table, her voice barely a whisper. "I can't stop seeing it. Cara, lying there… it's my fault."

"It's not," Marianne said firmly, reaching across to take her hand. "You didn't put that knife in the attacker's hand. You didn't choose violence—they did."

"But I dragged her into this," Ginger argued, tears brimming in her green eyes. "I thought I could handle it. That I could solve this mystery and keep everyone safe. I was wrong."

Marianne's grip tightened. "You're not wrong to want justice, Ginger. And you're not wrong to fight for the people you care about. That's who you are. Don't let this make you doubt that."

Ginger bit her lip, staring into her mother's unwavering gaze. Her words resonated, but the doubt lingered, a heavy shadow she couldn't shake.

Upstairs, Ginger's bedroom became her war room. The note she'd found at the warehouse lay spread across her desk, alongside clippings from old newspapers, maps of the town, and her own scribbled notes. Every thread seemed tangled, every lead fraught with danger.

She stared at the confession in her hand, the warning chillingly clear: *"Stay out, or you'll regret it."*

"Not a chance," Ginger muttered under her breath.

A knock at the door startled her. Dan stepped inside, his expression guarded. "Mind if I join?"

Ginger hesitated, then nodded. "I could use another set of eyes."

Ginger Snapped

For the next hour, they pored over the evidence together. Dan's sharp mind brought clarity to details Ginger had overlooked, but her intuition led them to connections he hadn't considered. By the time midnight struck, they had a clearer picture of the attacker's potential motives—but more questions than answers.

As Dan rose to leave, he paused at the door. "You've got guts, Ginger. And a brain to match. Don't let today shake that."

She met his gaze, a flicker of gratitude in her eyes. "Thanks, Dan."

When he left, Ginger turned back to her desk. Her resolve had crystallized. This wasn't just about solving Edith's murder anymore. It was about protecting everyone she loved—and making sure no one else got hurt.

She wouldn't stop. Not until the killer was behind bars.

Chapter 6

The warm scent of vanilla and cinnamon lingered in the air, comforting but unable to mask the bitter reality that had settled over Ginger's bakery. Evidence bags cluttered the counter, a grim reminder of the murder that had shattered the peaceful rhythm of her life. Determination flickered in her eyes as she stood beside Dan, the police detective who had unexpectedly become her ally.

Ginger's fingers brushed against the delivery schedule pinned to the corkboard. "Look at this, Dan. This sugar delivery… it's marked for Tuesday, but we didn't get it until Thursday. And Mrs. Henderson was here Wednesday morning."

Dan leaned in, his presence steadying. "You think there's a connection?"

Ginger's mind raced. "Maybe. Or maybe whoever tampered with the schedule didn't count on me keeping such detailed records." She shot him a small, wry smile. "Bakers have to be precise."

"Then let's dig into it," Dan said, his voice a quiet reassurance. "Who handles your deliveries?"

"Two companies, but this one—" she tapped the invoice again, "—it's local. They've been reliable until now."

Dan pulled out his notepad. "Let's pay them a visit. If someone's messing with your deliveries, they might know something."

The suggestion felt like a lifeline. Ginger grabbed her coat, determination replacing the hesitation that had clouded her thoughts. As they stepped outside, the crisp autumn air carried the faintest hint of rain, a stark contrast to the cozy warmth of the bakery.

The delivery company's office was tucked away in a nondescript industrial park on the edge of town. Ginger's nerves prickled as they approached the door, its peeling paint a testament to years of neglect. Dan knocked firmly, and after a moment, a wiry man with a clipboard opened it.

"Can I help you?" the man asked, his tone wary.

Dan flashed his badge. "Detective Griffith. This is Ginger Lawrence. We have some questions about a recent delivery to her bakery."

The man's gaze flickered between them. "Uh, sure. Come in."

The office smelled faintly of motor oil and stale coffee. Ginger's eyes scanned the room, landing on a corkboard cluttered with papers and a whiteboard listing delivery schedules. She stepped closer, her pulse quickening as she spotted her bakery's name.

"What's this?" Ginger asked, pointing at the board. "It says the sugar delivery was completed on Tuesday."

The man frowned. "That's what our driver logged."

Dan's voice was sharp. "Can we speak to the driver?"

The man hesitated, then nodded. "Wait here." He disappeared through a side door, leaving Ginger and Dan alone.

Ginger whispered, "Something's off. If the delivery was logged, why didn't I get it until Thursday?"

Dan's eyes narrowed. "We'll find out."

The driver appeared moments later, a burly man with a scruffy beard. His eyes darted nervously as he entered. "What's this about?"

Dan stepped forward. "Your delivery to Ginger's bakery this past week. Did you drop it off on Tuesday as scheduled?"

The man rubbed the back of his neck. "Uh, yeah. I think so."

Ginger crossed her arms. "You think? Or you know?"

The driver's gaze dropped. "Look, it was a busy day. Maybe I… got the days mixed up."

Dan's tone turned icy. "You're aware there's an ongoing murder investigation tied to this case?"

The driver paled. "M-murder?"

"That's right," Dan said. "So if you've got anything to share, now's the time."

Sweat beaded on the driver's forehead. "I swear, I'm not involved. But... there was something weird that day. A guy stopped me near the bakery. Said he'd handle the delivery."

Ginger's heart pounded. "What did he look like?"

"Tall, dark hair, wearing a brown jacket. Didn't give his name. Just handed me some cash and told me to take the rest of the day off."

Dan's jaw tightened. "And you didn't think to report this?"

The driver shrugged helplessly. "It didn't seem like a big deal at the time."

Ginger's stomach churned. "He could be the killer."

Dan placed a reassuring hand on her arm. "We'll track him down. Let's get back to the station and run a description."

Hours later, Ginger sat in the station's small conference room, her nerves fraying as the clock ticked. Dan returned, a file in hand.

"We've got a lead," he said, his voice steady. "The description matches a man named Colin Reilly. He's got a record—petty theft, breaking and entering. Lives on the outskirts of town."

Ginger's throat tightened. "What would he want with my bakery?"

Dan's expression darkened. "We're going to find out. But I need you to stay here, Ginger. Let me handle this."

Her protest died on her lips as she saw the concern in his eyes. "Alright," she whispered. "Be careful."

The next hour felt like an eternity. Ginger paced the room, her mind racing with worst-case scenarios. When the door finally opened, Dan stepped inside, his expression grim but resolute.

"We found him," he said. "And we found this." He placed a small, bloodstained cloth on the table. "It was in his jacket pocket. Matches the blood type from the bakery."

Ginger's breath caught. "So he did it?"

"He's not talking yet," Dan said. "But it's a start. We'll keep pressing him."

Relief mingled with lingering fear. "Thank you, Dan. For everything."

He gave her a small, reassuring smile. "We're not done yet, but we're getting closer."

Ginger nodded, determination returning. "Together?"

Dan's eyes softened. "Together."

Ginger Snapped

As they prepared to face the next steps, Ginger felt the spark of hope reignite. She wasn't alone in this fight. With Dan by her side, she'd see it through to the end.

Chapter 6

Ginger's fingers trembled as she ran them along the edge of Mary's desk. A faint click. Her heart raced.

"What the..."

A hidden compartment sprang open, revealing a stack of yellowed envelopes. Ginger's eyes widened as she read the name scrawled across the top one: Edith Fernwood.

She glanced at the office door, listening for footsteps. Silence. With shaking hands, she opened the first letter.

"Dear Edith,

The plan is in motion. We must act swiftly..."

Ginger's breath caught. She scanned further, her mind reeling.

"This can't be real."

But as she devoured letter after letter, the truth became undeniable. Mary and Edith, conspiring together. But for what?

"Oh my god."

The final letter spelled it out clearly. A plot that went deeper than she could have imagined. Ginger's legs wobbled, and she gripped the desk for support.

"How could they?"

Her mind flashed to Mary's warm smile, her comforting presence in the cafe. It had all been a lie.

Ginger's shock gave way to determination. She had to expose this, clear her name. But how?

She carefully replaced the letters, her baker's hands steady despite her racing thoughts. As she closed the compartment, a plan began to form.

Ginger Snapped

"I'll make this right," she whispered. "For all of us."

Ginger fumbled for her phone, her flour-dusted fingers leaving smudges on the screen. She hit Cara's number first.

"Cara, it's me. You won't believe what I found."

"Ginger? What's wrong? You sound—"

"No time. Call Dan. Meet me at the bakery. It's urgent."

She ended the call and dialed Detective Griffith.

"Detective, I've got evidence. Mary and Edith—they were working together."

"Slow down, Ginger. What are you talking about?"

"Letters. A hidden compartment. It's all here."

"Don't touch anything else. I'm on my way."

Ginger paced the length of her bakery, the scent of cinnamon and vanilla usually comforting, now cloying. The bell above the door jingled.

Cara rushed in, her brown eyes wide with concern. "Ginger, what's going on?"

Before Ginger could answer, Detective Griffith strode in, his presence filling the small space.

"Alright, Lawrence. Let's hear it."

Ginger took a deep breath, her freckled hands clenching and unclenching. "I found letters. Mary and Edith were conspiring together."

Dan's eyes narrowed. "That's a serious accusation."

"I know what I saw."

Cara placed a gentle hand on Ginger's arm. "Start from the beginning."

Ginger nodded, her red hair falling into her eyes as she recounted her discovery. With each detail, Dan's expression grew more intense, while Cara's softened with understanding.

"We need to confront Mary," Ginger concluded.

Dan shook his head. "It's not that simple. We need—"

"What we need is to act now," Ginger interrupted, her green eyes flashing. "Before she destroys any more evidence."

Cara's quiet voice cut through the tension. "Perhaps we should consider all our options."

Ginger's jaw clenched. "I'm done waiting. I'm going to confront Mary myself."

Dan stepped forward, his brow furrowed. "That's too risky, Ginger. We don't know what she's capable of."

"I don't care. This ends now." Ginger's voice trembled with determination.

Cara's gentle tone carried a note of concern. "Ginger, please think this through. Your safety—"

"My safety?" Ginger laughed bitterly. "What about my reputation? My business? My life?"

Dan ran a hand through his hair. "I understand your frustration, but—"

"No, you don't." Ginger's eyes blazed. "This is my fight. I need to face her."

Cara and Dan exchanged worried glances.

"At least let us come with you," Cara pleaded.

Ginger hesitated, then nodded. "Fine. But I do the talking."

Dan sighed heavily. "I can't believe I'm agreeing to this."

"Then don't," Ginger snapped. "I'll go alone if I have to."

"Like hell you will," Dan growled. "We're in this together."

Cara squeezed Ginger's hand. "Always."

Ginger took a deep breath, her resolve hardening. "Then let's go catch a killer."

Ginger's kitchen bustled with nervous energy as the trio prepared for their confrontation with Mary. Dan spread a manila folder across the flour-dusted countertop, his piercing blue eyes scanning the documents within.

"We need to organize this evidence meticulously," he muttered, arranging photos and letters.

Cara's gentle voice chimed in. "What about the security footage from the bakery?"

"Good thinking." Ginger rummaged through a drawer, producing a small USB drive. "It's all here."

Dan nodded approvingly. "That could be crucial."

Ginger's hands trembled slightly as she packed the evidence into her messenger bag. Her heart raced, a mix of determination and fear coursing through her veins.

"You okay?" Cara's soft touch on her arm startled her.

"Fine," Ginger lied, forcing a smile. "Just ready to end this."

The drive to Mary's café felt interminable. Ginger's fingers tapped an anxious rhythm on the steering wheel, her eyes darting to the rearview mirror where Dan's car followed closely.

"What if we're wrong?" she whispered, doubt creeping into her voice.

Cara squeezed her hand. "We're not. The evidence is clear."

As they approached the café, Ginger's stomach churned. The familiar storefront loomed ahead, now ominous and foreboding.

"This is it," she breathed, parking the car with shaking hands.

Dan's gruff voice came from behind as he approached. "Remember, we're right here with you."

Ginger nodded, squaring her shoulders. "Let's finish this."

The bell above the door chimed as Ginger pushed it open, her heart pounding. The aroma of fresh coffee and baked goods hit her, a stark contrast to the tension in her body.

Mary looked up from behind the counter, her smile faltering. "Ginger? What brings you here?"

Ginger's voice wavered slightly. "We need to talk, Mary."

Dan and Cara flanked her, their presence reassuring.

Mary's eyes darted between them. "Is everything alright?"

Ginger took a deep breath, her fingers clutching the strap of her messenger bag. "No, it's not. We know about the letters, Mary."

Mary's face paled. "What letters?"

Ginger pulled out the stack of correspondence. "These. Between you and Edith Fernwood."

Mary's hands trembled as she reached for them. "Where did you-"

"That's not important." Ginger's voice grew stronger. "What matters is what's in them. You were involved in Edith's murder, weren't you?"

The café fell silent. A customer at a nearby table stopped mid-sip, eyes wide.

Mary's voice was barely audible. "Ginger, you don't understand-"

"Then help me understand." Ginger leaned forward, her green eyes intense. "Because right now, all evidence points to you."

Dan cleared his throat. "Mrs. Ashton, I suggest you explain yourself."

Cara's soft voice added, "We're here to listen, Mary. But we need the truth."

Ginger's heart raced as she waited for Mary's response, the weight of the moment heavy in the air.

Mary's fingers clutched the edge of the counter, knuckles white. "This is ridiculous. I've known Edith for years. Why would I-"

"The letters, Mary." Ginger's voice hardened. "They speak for themselves."

Mary's eyes darted to the exit. "You're misinterpreting things."

Ginger slammed her palm on the counter. "Am I? Then explain the coded messages about 'silencing the problem'."

A gasp from a nearby customer. Mary flinched.

"I-I can't discuss this here." Mary's voice quavered.

Ginger leaned in closer. "You don't have a choice anymore."

Mary's composure cracked. "You don't know what you're talking about!"

"Then enlighten me!" Ginger's voice rose. "Because right now, you look guilty as hell."

Mary's eyes flashed. "Watch your tone, young lady."

"Or what?" Ginger challenged. "You'll silence me too?"

The café fell deathly quiet. Mary's face contorted.

"How dare you-" Mary's voice cracked.

Ginger pressed on. "The truth, Mary. Now."

Mary's breath came in short gasps. "I never meant for anyone to get hurt."

Ginger's heart pounded. She was close to breaking through.

"What did you mean then?" Ginger demanded.

Mary's eyes welled with tears. "You don't understand the pressure I was under."

Ginger softened her tone. "Then help me understand, Mary. Please."

Detective Dan Griffith stepped forward, his piercing blue eyes scanning the tense scene. He placed a steady hand on Ginger's shoulder.

"Let's take a breath here," Dan's deep voice cut through the tension. "Mary, we need to have this conversation, but let's move it somewhere more private."

Ginger's chest heaved as she fought to control her emotions. She nodded, grateful for Dan's intervention.

"My office," Mary whispered, her earlier bravado crumbling.

Dan guided them to the back, his presence a calming force. "Now, Mary, we're here to listen. Take your time and tell us what happened."

Ginger Snapped

Mary sank into her chair, shoulders slumping. "It was never supposed to go this far."

Ginger perched on the edge of her seat, heart racing. "What wasn't?"

"The blackmail," Mary's voice cracked. "Edith... she found out about my past. Threatened to expose everything."

Dan leaned forward, his tone measured. "What past, Mary?"

Mary's eyes glistened. "Before Haversham Falls, I... I embezzled money from my previous employer. Edith discovered it."

Ginger's mind reeled. "So you killed her to keep her quiet?"

"No!" Mary's head snapped up. "I mean... not directly. I hired someone to scare her, to get the evidence. But it went wrong."

Dan's jaw tightened. "Who did you hire?"

Mary's shoulders shook as she sobbed. "A man named Joey. He was supposed to break in, find the documents. But Edith caught him, and he panicked."

Ginger felt sick. "And you covered it up?"

Mary nodded, defeat etched on her face. "I was terrified. I thought I could make it all go away."

Dan's voice was steady. "We're going to need all the details, Mary. From the beginning."

As Mary began her confession, Ginger's mind whirled. The warmth and kindness she'd always associated with Mary seemed to evaporate, leaving behind a stranger she barely recognized.

Ginger's hands trembled as she reached for her phone. "I'm calling the sheriff."

Dan nodded, his eyes never leaving Mary. "Good call."

Cara squeezed Ginger's arm. "It's over, Gin. You're cleared."

Mary's sobs echoed through the cafe. "I'm so sorry. I never meant —"

"Save it for the judge," Dan cut in, voice hard.

Ginger's fingers shook as she dialed. The phone rang once, twice —

"Sheriff's office."

"It's Ginger Lawrence. We need you at Mary's Cafe. Now."

She hung up, heart pounding. Dan was already moving, pulling out his handcuffs.

"Mary Ashton, you're under arrest for conspiracy to commit murder and obstruction of justice."

The metal clinked as he secured Mary's wrists. Ginger watched, a mix of relief and sadness washing over her.

Cara's arm wrapped around her shoulders. "You did it, Gin. You solved it."

Ginger leaned into her friend's embrace. "We did it. I couldn't have —"

The cafe door burst open. Sheriff Johnson strode in, taking in the scene.

"Detective Griffith? What's going on here?"

Dan straightened. "Mary Ashton just confessed to her involvement in Edith Fernwood's murder."

The sheriff's eyebrows shot up. "Well, I'll be damned."

As Dan filled him in, Ginger's gaze drifted to Mary. The woman who'd been her mentor, her friend, now sat defeated and small.

"I trusted you," Ginger whispered.

Mary's tear-filled eyes met hers. "I know. I'm so—"

Ginger turned away, unable to bear it. Cara's grip tightened.

"Let's go home, Gin. It's over."

As they stepped out into the crisp evening air, Ginger took a deep breath. For the first time in weeks, she felt the weight lift from her shoulders.

Justice would be served. Her name was cleared. And tomorrow... tomorrow she'd bake again.

Chapter 6 ★

The bell above the cafe door jingled as Ginger and Dan stepped inside, the sound breaking the stillness of the chilly afternoon. A wave of warmth enveloped them, carrying the comforting scent of cinnamon, freshly baked scones, and rich coffee. It was a stark contrast to the biting wind outside, but something in the air felt...off.

Ginger's keen eyes swept across the quaint interior. The rustic wooden tables were set with their usual cheery yellow napkins, and the sunlight streaming through the windows bathed the cafe in a golden glow. Yet, the place felt unnaturally still. Behind the counter, Mary was vigorously polishing the espresso machine, but her movements lacked their usual grace. Her hands trembled, and the cloth slipped from her grasp, falling to the floor.

"Something's not right," Ginger murmured under her breath.

Dan, ever the stoic detective, tightened his jaw. "Stay alert."

The pair approached the counter slowly, their boots scuffing against the wooden floor. Mary's head jerked up at the sound, and for a fleeting moment, her eyes widened in what could only be described as panic. She quickly masked her expression with a forced smile.

"Ginger! Detective Griffith!" Mary greeted, her voice unnaturally high-pitched. "What a lovely surprise. What can I get for you two?"

Her hands twisted the hem of her apron nervously, and Ginger's heart clenched. This wasn't the Mary she knew—warm, unflappable Mary who always had a kind word and a ready laugh. Something had shaken her deeply.

"Just stopping by to chat," Dan said evenly, his piercing blue gaze never leaving Mary's face.

Mary's smile faltered, and her eyes darted toward the clock on the wall as if searching for an escape. "Oh? What about?" she asked, her voice wavering.

Ginger leaned in, her tone gentle but firm. "Is everything okay, Mary? You seem a bit... off."

Mary's grip on the counter tightened, her knuckles turning white. For a moment, it seemed she might confide in them, but then she shook her head and forced another smile.

"Just a bit tired, dear. Nothing to worry about," she replied, but her voice betrayed her unease.

Ginger exchanged a quick glance with Dan, whose sharp eyes were already assessing every detail of Mary's behavior.

"Are you sure?" Ginger pressed softly. "You know you can talk to us about anything."

Mary's hands twisted a dishcloth anxiously. "It's nothing, really," she insisted. "Now, how about some fresh scones? They just came out of the oven."

The overly bright tone set off alarm bells in Ginger's mind. Mary was deflecting, and she was doing a poor job of it. Ginger glanced at Dan again, and the unspoken agreement between them was clear: they weren't leaving without answers.

"Mary," Ginger said, her voice firm but kind, "we need to talk. It's important."

Mary's smile wavered, and her eyes darted between Ginger and Dan. "Can't it wait, dear? I've got a batch of—"

"I'm afraid it can't," Dan interrupted, his tone calm but resolute.

Mary's shoulders sagged, and the facade she had so carefully maintained began to crumble. "Alright," she said softly. "Let me just close up for a bit."

As Mary moved to flip the "Open" sign to "Closed," Ginger caught Dan's eye. His lips were pressed into a thin line, his gaze never wavering from Mary. The tension in the room was palpable.

"Ready for anything?" Ginger whispered.

Dan gave a curt nod. "Always."

Mary locked the door and turned to face them, her eyes glistening with unshed tears. The cafe, usually a haven of warmth and comfort, now felt stiflingly small. Ginger's stomach churned as she took a deep breath, bracing herself for what was to come.

"Mary," she began gently, "we need to know the truth about Edith's murder. What really happened that night?"

Mary's eyes widened in panic, and her hands flew to her mouth. She took a step back, shaking her head.

"I... I don't know what you're talking about," she stammered, her voice barely above a whisper.

Ginger stepped closer, her green eyes filled with determination. "Please, Mary. We know you were there. We just want to understand."

Mary's composure cracked, and she began to tremble. "It was an accident," she whispered, her voice choked with emotion. "I swear, I never meant to..."

She broke off, her sobs filling the silence. Ginger's heart ached for her friend, but she knew they couldn't stop now. They were too close to the truth.

"Never meant to what, Mary?" Dan's voice was low, steady, and filled with quiet authority.

Mary's gaze darted around the room, searching for an escape that didn't exist. Her chest heaved with panicked breaths as she clutched the counter for support.

"I didn't mean to hurt her," Mary finally choked out, tears streaming down her face. "I just wanted her to stop."

Ginger's heart pounded in her chest. "What happened, Mary?" she asked softly.

Mary's voice was barely audible as she began to speak. "Edith found out... about the money. The cafe was failing, and I was desperate. I started laundering money to keep it afloat. She threatened to expose me."

Dan's jaw tightened, but his voice remained calm. "And what happened that night?"

Mary's hands shook as she wiped her tears. "We argued. She said she was going to the police. I panicked. I pushed her, and she fell. She hit her head on the counter."

Ginger swallowed hard, her throat dry. "And then?"

Mary's voice broke. "I staged it to look like an accident. I was so scared. I didn't know what else to do."

The weight of her confession hung heavy in the air. Ginger's chest tightened as she glanced at Dan. His expression was a mix of sadness and resolve.

"Mary," Dan said gently, stepping forward, "I have to take you into custody."

Mary nodded slowly, her face a mask of guilt and despair. "I understand," she whispered.

Dan reached for his handcuffs, his movements careful and measured. As he secured them around Mary's wrists, Ginger placed a comforting hand on her friend's shoulder.

"You did the right thing by telling the truth," Ginger said softly. "We'll make sure you're treated fairly."

Mary's tear-streaked face turned toward Ginger, a flicker of gratitude in her eyes. "Thank you," she murmured. "For believing in me."

As they guided Mary out of the cafe, the bright sunlight outside felt almost surreal. A small crowd had gathered, their curious whispers filling the air. Ginger held her head high, determined to shield Mary from their judgmental stares.

"It's not the end, Mary," Ginger said firmly as they walked toward the waiting police car. "It's just the beginning of making things right."

Dan opened the car door, his movements steady and respectful. Mary hesitated for a moment before stepping inside, her shoulders slumping with the weight of her actions.

As the car pulled away, Ginger stood on the sidewalk, her heart heavy. The truth had come to light, but the cost was steep. She glanced back at the cafe, its cheerful yellow facade now seeming somber and muted.

"Haversham Falls will heal," Dan said quietly, his voice filled with quiet conviction. "It always does."

Ginger nodded, a faint smile tugging at her lips. "And so will Mary. She's stronger than she thinks."

Together, they turned and walked away, the promise of justice and healing guiding their steps.

Chapter 68

Ginger's heart thundered in her chest as she pushed open the swinging door to Mary's café kitchen. The warm, inviting scent of freshly baked bread wrapped around her like a deceptive comfort, clashing with the crackling tension in the air. Her pulse raced, each step forward feeling like a leap across a yawning chasm.

Dan stood solidly behind her, his calm presence a quiet anchor. She could feel his steadying energy even without looking. It was the only thing keeping her from losing her nerve.

Mary turned sharply from the prep table, where she'd been slicing a loaf of her signature sourdough. Her expression flickered between surprise and irritation before settling on a carefully neutral mask.

"Ginger," Mary said with forced brightness, her knife poised mid-slice. "What brings you here? Baking tips, perhaps?"

Ginger's fists clenched at her sides. She forced herself to speak, her voice sharper than she intended. "Mary, we need to talk. About Edith."

Mary's smile faltered, her grip tightening on the knife handle. "What about her? Such a tragedy. I still can't believe she's gone."

Ginger's jaw tightened. She took a step closer, planting herself firmly across the stainless steel prep table from Mary. "You know exactly what about. Let's not pretend, Mary."

Dan moved to stand beside Ginger, his blue eyes locked on Mary's every movement. "We have questions about your involvement in Edith's death."

Mary's face drained of color, her free hand trembling slightly as it rested against the counter. "My involvement?" she repeated, her voice high-pitched and incredulous. "That's absurd! I would never hurt Edith."

"Stop lying," Ginger snapped, her voice rising. "We know you had motive."

Mary's eyes darted between them, her calm composure fraying. "Motive?" she stammered. "What possible reason would I have to kill her?"

Dan leaned forward, his voice low and unyielding. "That's what we're here to find out."

For a moment, the kitchen was silent except for the hum of the refrigerator and the faint ticking of a wall clock. Then Mary's composure cracked. Her lips curled into a snarl as she jabbed a finger in Ginger's direction.

"If anyone had reason to want Edith dead, it was you, Ginger!" Mary's voice was sharp, cutting through the tension like a blade. "Everyone knows you two were rivals."

The accusation hit Ginger like a slap, but she recovered quickly, her green eyes blazing. "How dare you try to pin this on me! I would never stoop to something so vile."

"No?" Mary shot back. "You've been gunning for my business for years, trying to steal my customers with your fancy pastries and glossy smiles."

Dan's hand touched Ginger's arm, grounding her. "Nice try, Mary, but deflecting won't work. We have evidence."

Mary's bravado faltered, her eyes widening. "Evidence?" she echoed, her voice barely above a whisper. "That's impossible."

Ginger took a deep breath, steadying her voice as she reached into her bag. She pulled out a folder and spread its contents across the table. The papers, creased from hours of handling, bore undeniable proof.

"Your financial records," Ginger began, tapping a highlighted line. "Show large withdrawals coinciding with Edith's... requests."

Mary's face twisted, her mouth opening and closing like a fish gasping for air.

"And this," Ginger continued, sliding another document forward, "is the threatening note Edith sent you. We had it analyzed. Your fingerprints were all over it."

Dan stepped closer, his sharp gaze observing every nuance of Mary's reaction. Her left eye twitched, her breathing quickened—telltale signs of a guilty conscience.

"You had no right to dig into my personal life," Mary hissed, her voice trembling with barely suppressed rage.

"We had every right," Dan countered, his voice firm and steady. "This is a murder investigation."

Ginger pressed on, her voice growing stronger. "And the poison? Traces of it were found here, in your kitchen. The same unique blend you use in your—"

"Secret recipe scones," Dan finished grimly.

The room fell silent again, the weight of their words settling over them like a heavy fog. Mary's trembling hand finally released the knife, letting it clatter to the counter. Her shoulders sagged, her eyes distant and filled with a mixture of anger and despair.

"You don't understand," Mary whispered, her voice barely audible. "None of you do."

Dan's jaw tightened. "Then help us understand. Why did you do it?"

Mary's head snapped up, her gaze burning with sudden fury. "Because that witch was going to destroy me!" she spat. "Edith found out about the money. She threatened to tell everyone unless I... paid her off."

Ginger's stomach churned. "The money from the café?"

Mary nodded, her voice breaking. "I was in debt. Deep debt. The café was struggling, and I... I thought I could fix it. But Edith found out. She said she'd ruin me. I just needed more time to pay it back."

"So you poisoned her," Dan said, his voice cold as ice. "To keep her quiet."

Mary's lip quivered, tears streaming down her face. "I didn't mean for it to go this far. I just... I panicked."

"It's over, Mary," Ginger said softly. "You need to face the consequences."

Dan stepped forward, his handcuffs glinting in the fluorescent light. "Mary Ashton, you're under arrest for the murder of Edith Holloway."

As he reached for her hands, Mary's gaze darted to the counter. In a flash, she lunged, snatching a second knife.

"Dan, look out!" Ginger screamed.

Dan reacted instantly, twisting away as the blade sliced the air where he'd been standing.

"Drop it, Mary!" Dan barked, his voice a commanding roar.

Mary's wild eyes flickered with desperation, but her grip on the knife wavered. Ginger edged closer, her pulse hammering in her ears.

"It's over, Mary," Ginger said gently, her voice steady despite the chaos. "You don't have to fight anymore."

Mary's body sagged, the knife slipping from her fingers and clattering to the floor. She crumpled to her knees, sobbing uncontrollably.

"I… I didn't want this," she whispered. "I didn't want any of this."

Dan quickly cuffed her, his movements efficient but not rough. "Mary Ashton, you're under arrest," he repeated.

As the wail of approaching sirens filled the air, Ginger felt her knees weaken. She leaned against the prep table, the cold metal grounding her.

"You okay?" Dan's voice was gruff, his blue eyes searching hers.

Ginger nodded, her voice trembling. "I think so. It's just… a lot."

Dan's hand brushed her arm, a gentle reassurance. "You did good, Ginger. Real good."

The warmth of his words settled in her chest, chasing away the lingering chill of fear. Together, they watched as the officers escorted Mary out, her sobs echoing faintly.

Ginger turned to Dan, her green eyes meeting his steady blue ones. "Thank you," she said softly.

He smiled, a rare, genuine smile that made her heart skip a beat. "We make a good team."

As the café door swung shut behind the officers, Ginger let out a long breath. The nightmare was over. Or so she hoped.

Chapter 1

Ginger's hands trembled as she fumbled with the keys outside her beloved bakery, *Ginger Snaps*. The wooden sign above the door, painted with whimsical lettering, swung gently in the cool morning breeze. The familiar scent of cinnamon and vanilla, carried on the air from the bakery's walls and her own memories, enveloped her like a warm embrace. It was a smell that reminded her of simpler times when her biggest worry was whether she'd burn the last batch of cookies. Now, it seemed to hold the weight of her future.

"You can do this," she whispered to herself, her voice barely audible over the rustling leaves on the cobblestone street of Haversham Falls. Her fingers finally found the right key, its brass surface cool and solid in her palm.

The lock clicked open with a sound that echoed in her chest. Ginger hesitated, her heart pounding so loudly she could feel it in her throat. She glanced at the reflection in the glass door: her own freckled face stared back, pale but determined, framed by unruly red curls she hadn't bothered to tame. The green eyes she inherited from her mother looked almost too bright, as if refusing to betray her fears. Was she ready to face everyone again? To see their eyes full of pity—or worse, suspicion—after everything that had happened?

She shook her head, forcing the doubts away. "No time for that now."

Pushing open the door, Ginger stepped inside. The scent of her bakery rushed to greet her, sweeter and warmer than she remembered.

Sunlight streamed through the windows, dancing across the wooden floors and gleaming display cases. The cases were empty now, but soon they'd be filled with her creations once again. Her eyes swept the room, taking in the copper pots hanging from their hooks, the cheerful curtains she'd sewn herself, and the small chalkboard sign behind the counter that read, "Baking Love Daily."

Her apron hung on its usual hook near the kitchen door. She reached for it, tying the soft fabric around her waist with practiced ease. The act was grounding, like slipping back into a role she was born to play. The apron felt like armor, shielding her from the lingering whispers that had haunted her dreams.

Her gaze landed on the "Closed" sign in the window. Her stomach churned at the sight. Flipping that sign was more than a formality—it was a declaration. A promise to herself and the town that she wasn't going anywhere. Ginger crossed the room, each step measured and deliberate, until she stood before the sign.

"This is it," she murmured, her fingers curling around the edge of the wooden plaque. With a deep breath, she flipped it over. The word "Open" now faced the world outside, a bold beacon to the people of Haversham Falls.

Stepping back, Ginger allowed herself a small smile. "Welcome back, old friend."

The sound of voices drifted through the partially open door, drawing her attention. She peeked outside and froze. A small crowd had gathered on the sidewalk, their faces lit with curiosity and anticipation. Among them, Mrs. Finch, the town librarian, waved enthusiastically, her knitted scarf trailing in the breeze.

"Look, everyone! She's open!" Mrs. Finch exclaimed, her voice cutting through the crisp morning air.

"About time!" Mr. Rodriguez, the retired mailman, chimed in with a grin. "I've been dreaming about those cinnamon rolls."

Ginger's chest tightened. She hadn't expected such a warm reception, especially after the events of the last few months. The shadow of that awful day still lingered in Haversham Falls, and she feared it would cling to her like flour on her apron. Yet, here they were—her neighbors, her friends—gathered with smiles that carried no judgment, only support.

Ginger Snapped

Squaring her shoulders, Ginger opened the door fully and stepped outside. The sunlight hit her face, and for a moment, she felt like a seedling breaking through the earth, reaching for something brighter.

"Good morning, everyone!" Her voice wavered slightly, but the smile she wore was genuine.

A ripple of chatter and laughter surged through the group as they moved closer, filling the bakery with their warmth. Ginger greeted each familiar face, her hands shaking less with every handshake, every kind word.

"Mrs. Finch, how lovely to see you," Ginger said, her cheeks flushing with emotion.

"Welcome back, dear," Mrs. Finch replied, squeezing Ginger's hand tightly. "We've missed you terribly."

"Mr. Rodriguez, your favorite cinnamon rolls will be out in no time."

"You're a lifesaver," he said with a wink.

As the morning wore on, the bakery buzzed with life. Ginger moved behind the counter, her hands instinctively finding the rhythm of her work. The smell of gingerbread and vanilla swirled through the air as she rolled dough, her movements precise and confident.

"Those smell heavenly, Ginger!" Mrs. Finch called from her seat near the window. She was sipping coffee from one of the bakery's blue ceramic mugs, her eyes twinkling.

Ginger chuckled, dusting flour from her hands. "Secret ingredient is love. And maybe just a pinch of sheer determination."

"Whatever it is, don't stop," Mr. Rodriguez added, savoring a bite of his cinnamon roll. "This is perfection."

The warmth of their praise filled Ginger with a renewed sense of purpose. This was why she baked—not for the accolades, but for the joy it brought others. For the sense of community that filled her bakery like the aroma of freshly baked cookies.

The bell above the door chimed again, and Ginger looked up to see her best friend, Cara Noonan, breezing in. Cara's auburn hair was tucked under a knitted hat, her cheeks rosy from the chill.

"Ginger!" Cara exclaimed, her voice bubbling with excitement. "This place is packed! You're killing it."

Ginger's heart swelled. "Cara, you made it."

"As if I'd miss this," Cara said, pulling her into a tight hug. "Need an extra pair of hands?"

"Always." Ginger handed her an apron. "Think you can handle the register?"

"Consider it done," Cara replied, tying the apron with a flourish.

They worked side by side, the hum of the bakery settling into a steady rhythm. Every now and then, Cara would lean over and whisper, "You're crushing it," or "Look at that line, Ging!" It was the kind of support Ginger hadn't realized she'd been craving.

The bell jingled again, and Ginger's breath caught when she saw her parents walk in. Her mother, Marianne, wore a soft cardigan that matched her silver-streaked hair, and her father, Nate, stood tall beside her, his weathered face breaking into a smile.

"Mom, Dad," Ginger said, her voice thick with emotion. She stepped from behind the counter, her hands nervously wringing her apron.

Her mother's eyes glistened. "Oh, sweetheart."

Nate placed a firm hand on her shoulder. "You've done good, kiddo."

"I'm sorry," Ginger blurted. "For pushing you away. For everything."

Marianne's hand found hers, squeezing gently. "No, love. We're sorry. We should have trusted you to find your way."

"And look at you now," Nate added. "You've built something wonderful."

Tears welled in Ginger's eyes. "I just wanted to make you proud."

Marianne smiled, her voice soft. "Ginger, we've always been proud of you. Even when things got hard."

Nate nodded. "Especially then."

They pulled her into a hug, the kind that made the world outside fade away. For the first time in months, Ginger felt like she could breathe again.

As the day wound down, the bakery quieted, leaving Ginger to clean up the counters and reflect. The bell jingled one last time, and she looked up to see Detective Dan Griffith walk in, his presence commanding the room.

"Looks like I missed the rush," he said, his blue eyes sparkling.

Ginger's heart skipped. "Dan. I mean, Detective Griffith. What brings you by?"

"Just checking on my favorite baker," he said, his smirk disarming. "And maybe snagging a cookie."

Ginger handed him a gingerbread man. Their fingers brushed, sending a spark through her that had nothing to do with static.

Dan took a bite, his expression lighting up. "This should be illegal. How is it so good?"

Ginger laughed, the sound surprising even her. "Trade secret."

"Well," Dan said, leaning in slightly, "if you ever feel like breaking a few more rules, let me know."

Their eyes met, and for a moment, the weight of the past few months melted away. In its place was something lighter, something that made Ginger think that maybe—just maybe—this was the beginning of something new.

Chapter 6

The bakery's warmth enveloped them, a stark contrast to the bitter cold outside. Ginger's fingers curled around her mug of hot cocoa, savoring its comforting heat. Across the small table, Detective Griffith mirrored her pose, his piercing blue eyes softening in the dim light.

Ginger inhaled deeply, the rich aroma of cocoa mingling with lingering notes of cinnamon and nutmeg from the day's baking. She glanced at the clock. Nearly midnight. Where had the time gone?

"Long day," Detective Griffith remarked, his deep voice cutting through the silence.

Ginger nodded. "But a productive one, thanks to you."

She studied his face, noting the fatigue etched in the lines around his eyes. Despite his gruff exterior, he'd been her rock throughout this ordeal. A wave of gratitude washed over her.

Detective Griffith took a sip of cocoa, leaving a faint mustache on his upper lip. Ginger stifled a smile.

"You've got a little..." She gestured to her own lip.

He wiped it away with the back of his hand. "Thanks."

Ginger's cheeks warmed, and she brushed a stray lock of hair behind her ear. Their eyes met, and her heart skipped a beat.

"Detective Griffith, I... I can't thank you enough for everything you've done."

He raised an eyebrow. "Just doing my job."

Ginger Snapped

Ginger shook her head. "No, it's more than that. You believed in me when no one else did. I couldn't have cleared my name without you."

Detective Griffith's expression softened. "You're tougher than you look, Miss Lawrence. Don't sell yourself short."

Ginger's lips curved into a grateful smile. She had misjudged him at first, thinking him cold and detached. Now she saw the compassion beneath his gruff exterior.

"Still, your support meant everything. I don't know how I would've gotten through this without you by my side."

Detective Griffith's blue eyes softened as he gazed at Ginger. He set his mug down with a gentle clink.

"I owe you an apology, Miss Lawrence."

Ginger's brow furrowed. "What for?"

"I misjudged you. Underestimated you." He leaned forward, elbows on the table. "Thought you were just another small-town baker in over her head."

Ginger's heart quickened. Was the stern detective actually admitting he'd been wrong?

"But now?" His voice lowered. "I see a remarkable woman. The strength you've shown... it's incredible."

Heat crept up Ginger's neck. She'd never heard him speak so candidly before.

"I..." She swallowed hard. "Thank you, Detective."

Without thinking, Ginger reached across the table. Her fingers brushed his hand, warm and calloused.

"Your support has meant everything," she said softly. "Your dedication, your unwavering pursuit of justice... I admire that so much."

Detective Griffith's gaze dropped to their hands, then back to her face. A hint of a smile played at his lips.

Ginger's pulse raced. What was happening between them? And more importantly – did she want it to stop?

Detective Griffith's thumb began to gently caress Ginger's hand. The small circular motion sent sparks through her body. He leaned in closer, his voice barely above a whisper.

"Ginger, I..." He paused, seemingly gathering courage. "I've developed deep feelings for you."

Her breath caught. Was this really happening?

"I can't imagine my life without you by my side anymore," he continued, his piercing blue eyes locked on hers.

Ginger's heart pounded. She felt dizzy, overwhelmed by the surge of emotion.

"Dan, I..." She struggled to find the right words. "I've fallen for you too."

His eyes widened slightly, a mix of relief and joy crossing his features.

"This connection between us," Ginger continued, her voice trembling slightly. "It's brought so much light into my life. Even with everything that's happened..."

Detective Griffith nodded, understanding in his gaze. "The investigation."

"Yes," Ginger breathed. "But you've been my anchor through it all."

She looked down at their intertwined hands, marveling at how natural it felt. When she looked back up, she found Dan's eyes still fixed on her, filled with warmth and something more. Something that made her heart race even faster.

Ginger's breath hitched as Dan leaned in closer. The scent of his cologne mingled with the lingering aroma of cocoa and fresh-baked gingerbread. Time seemed to slow as their lips met, soft and tentative at first.

Dan's hand cupped her cheek, his touch gentle yet electrifying. Ginger's eyes fluttered closed as she melted into the kiss, savoring the warmth that spread through her entire being.

The world around them faded away. The ticking of the bakery clock, the hum of the refrigerator, all of it vanished. There was only Dan, only this moment.

When they finally parted, Ginger's cheeks flushed a rosy pink. She opened her eyes to find Dan gazing at her, a shy smile playing at his lips.

"Wow," Dan breathed.

Ginger let out a soft laugh. "Yeah... wow."

Their hands remained intertwined on the table. Dan's thumb resumed its gentle caress of her skin.

"I've wanted to do that for a while now," he admitted.

"Me too," Ginger confessed. "I just wasn't sure if—"

"If I felt the same?" Dan finished for her.

She nodded, biting her lower lip.

"Ginger, you're... extraordinary. I've never met anyone quite like you."

Her heart swelled at his words. "Dan, I—"

The oven timer chimed, startling them both.

Ginger laughed, the spell momentarily broken. "Sorry, I forgot I had a batch in."

"Duty calls," Dan said with a grin. "But this... us... we're just getting started, aren't we?"

Ginger squeezed his hand. "Absolutely."

Ginger stood up, her fingers still intertwined with Dan's. "You know, we've been cooped up in here all day. How about we take a break and go for a walk in the park?"

Dan's eyes lit up. "I'd love that. It'd be nice to spend time together outside of... all this." He gestured vaguely at the bakery, a reminder of the investigation that had brought them together.

"Great!" Ginger beamed. "Let me just grab my coat."

As they stepped outside, the crisp winter air nipped at their cheeks. Dan instinctively reached for Ginger's hand, his larger one enveloping hers.

"Your hands are freezing," he remarked, concern lacing his voice.

Ginger chuckled. "Occupational hazard. I'm always washing them in cold water at the bakery."

Dan brought her hand to his lips, pressing a warm kiss to her knuckles. "Better?"

A pleasant shiver ran down Ginger's spine. "Much."

They strolled through the park, their breaths visible in the chilly air. The bare trees stood like sentinels, their branches reaching towards the steel-gray sky.

"So, Detective Griffith," Ginger teased, "what made you want to become a cop?"

Dan's eyes crinkled with amusement. "Back to formalities, are we? Well, Ms. Lawrence, if you must know, it was my grandfather. He was on the force for forty years."

"Really? That's amazing."

"Yeah, he was my hero growing up. Always told the best stories."

Ginger smiled, picturing a young Dan hanging on his grandfather's every word. "And what about you? Any childhood dreams of being a baker?"

Dan laughed, the sound rich and warm. "Not exactly. But I did have a mean sweet tooth. Still do, actually."

"Oh? I might have to put that to the test sometime."

As they rounded a bend in the path, a squirrel darted across their path, causing Ginger to jump slightly.

Dan's arm instinctively wrapped around her waist. "Whoa there. You okay?"

Ginger leaned into his embrace, relishing his warmth. "Yeah, just startled me. Thanks for the save, though."

They continued walking, Dan's arm remaining comfortably around her. Ginger felt a sense of peace wash over her, despite the turmoil of the past few days.

"You know," Dan said softly, "I'm really glad we're doing this. Getting to know each other outside of the case."

Ginger nodded, her heart full. "Me too, Dan. Me too."

As they approached the small gazebo, its white-painted wood gleaming in the afternoon sun, Ginger felt her heart quicken. She stopped, turning to face Dan, her green eyes meeting his piercing blue gaze.

"Dan, I..." Ginger paused, tucking a wayward strand of red hair behind her ear. "I can't thank you enough for everything you've done."

Dan's eyebrows furrowed slightly. "What do you mean?"

"Your support, your belief in me. It means more than you know." Ginger's voice softened, her fingers intertwining with his. "I'm excited for what's ahead - for us, both personally and professionally."

A slow smile spread across Dan's face, his eyes crinkling at the corners. He squeezed her hand gently.

"Ginger, I-" He cleared his throat, his usual brusqueness giving way to a rare vulnerability. "Being by your side, it's been... well, it's been an honor."

Ginger's breath caught in her throat. She'd never seen the detective so open before.

Dan continued, his voice low and sincere. "I'm looking forward to building a future together. One filled with love, trust, and-" He chuckled softly. "Maybe even a little adventure."

Ginger's heart soared. She'd faced countless challenges in recent days, but standing here with Dan, she felt ready to take on anything.

"Adventure, huh?" Ginger grinned, her eyes sparkling. "I hope you're ready for some baking experiments. I've got a new gingerbread recipe I've been dying to try."

Dan laughed, pulling her closer. "As long as I get to be your taste-tester, count me in."

Ginger's heart raced as Dan leaned in, his warm breath mingling with hers. Their lips met in a tender kiss, sealing their commitment. The world around them faded away, leaving only the two of them in this perfect moment.

Dan's strong arms encircled her waist, pulling her closer. Ginger's fingers traced the rough stubble along his jaw, reveling in the contrast against her baker's hands.

As they slowly parted, Ginger's cheeks flushed. "Wow," she breathed.

Dan's eyes sparkled with affection. "Wow indeed."

Hand in hand, they began the walk back to Ginger Snaps. The crisp air nipped at their cheeks, but Ginger felt warm from the inside out.

"You know," Dan mused, "when I first moved here, I never expected to find... this."

Ginger squeezed his hand. "What, a murder investigation?"

He chuckled. "No, a partner. Someone who challenges me, makes me better."

"We do make a good team," Ginger agreed. Her mind drifted to the obstacles they'd overcome. "Whatever comes next, we'll face it together."

Dan nodded, his expression determined. "Together."

As they approached the bakery, Ginger's excitement bubbled over. "Just wait until you try my new cinnamon rolls. They're to die for."

Dan groaned. "If I keep sampling your baking, I'll need a bigger uniform."

Ginger laughed, her eyes twinkling mischievously. "Don't worry, Detective. I'll keep you on your toes."

As they stepped into Ginger Snaps, the warm aroma of gingerbread enveloped them. Ginger inhaled deeply, her eyes closing in contentment.

Dan's hand tightened around hers. "Smells like home."

Ginger's heart skipped. She turned, meeting his gaze. "It does, doesn't it?"

They shared a smile, filled with promise and understanding.

Ginger reluctantly released his hand, moving behind the counter. "Let me grab those cinnamon rolls."

Dan leaned against the counter, watching her. "So, any new theories about Mrs. Abernathy's missing brooch?"

"Actually, yes." Ginger's brow furrowed as she plated the pastries. "I think we should talk to her gardener again."

"The quiet fellow with the limp?"

Ginger nodded, sliding the plate towards him. "He seemed nervous when we mentioned the timeline."

Dan took a bite, his eyes widening. "These are incredible. And you might be onto something with the gardener."

"See? Good food fuels good detective work."

He chuckled, reaching for her hand again. "What would I do without you, Ging?"

Ginger's heart swelled. Whatever challenges lay ahead, they'd face them together – one pastry at a time.

Chapter 6

Ginger's hands moved with practiced precision, sifting flour into the large mixing bowl. The comforting scent of cinnamon and nutmeg wafted through the kitchen.

"Almost ready," she murmured to herself.

Her eyes flicked to the window. A small crowd had gathered outside Ginger Snaps Bakery, their faces eager and expectant. Ginger's heart swelled with affection for her beloved town.

She cracked eggs into the bowl, whisking vigorously. "Time to show Haversham Falls what we're made of."

The rich molasses poured in a golden stream. Ginger inhaled deeply, savoring the aroma that spoke of home and comfort.

"You've got this, Ging," she said firmly. Her freckled nose crinkled as she smiled.

Outside, the townsfolk's excited chatter grew louder. Ginger could make out familiar voices - Mrs. Henderson's reedy tones, little Timmy's high-pitched giggle.

She dusted flour off her apron. "Just like riding a bike."

The dough came together smoothly under her expert touch. Ginger kneaded it gently, her movements sure and steady.

"Welcome back, old friend," she whispered.

A knock at the door made her jump. Ginger's best friend Cara poked her head in.

"You okay in here? The natives are getting restless."

Ginger grinned. "Tell them perfection takes time."

Cara laughed. "That's my girl. Need any help?"

"Nah, I've got this. But thanks."

As Cara left, Ginger shaped the dough into a ball. She felt a fierce surge of pride and determination.

"Alright, Haversham Falls," she said softly. "Let's show them what we're made of."

Ginger slid the trays of gingerbread men into the oven, her movements swift and practiced. The golden dough glistened under the bakery lights.

"In you go, little guys," she murmured, closing the oven door with a gentle click.

The warm, spicy aroma began wafting through the air. Ginger inhaled deeply, her eyes closing in bliss.

"Nothing beats that smell."

She turned, surveying the bakery. Bare walls and empty shelves stared back at her.

"Time for a makeover," Ginger declared, reaching for a box of decorations.

She unfurled a string of twinkling lights, their soft glow illuminating her determined expression.

"Let's bring some cheer back to this place."

As she worked, stringing lights and hanging banners, Ginger's mind wandered.

What if they don't come back? What if the scandal's ruined everything?

She shook her head firmly. "No. They're out there waiting. They believe in you."

The timer dinged. Ginger rushed to the oven, peeking inside.

"Perfect!" she exclaimed, pulling out the trays of perfectly baked gingerbread men.

Their sweet scent mingled with the pine of the garlands she'd hung. Ginger stood back, admiring her handiwork.

Colorful banners proclaimed "Welcome Back!" and "We Missed You!" Twinkling lights cast a warm glow over everything.

"Now that's more like it," she said, hands on her hips. "Haversham Falls, get ready for a celebration."

Ginger Snapped

A gentle knock on the bakery's front window startled Ginger. She turned to see her mother, Marianne, waving enthusiastically. Beside her stood Nate, his eyes crinkling with pride.

Ginger rushed to unlock the door. "Mom! Dad! You're early!"

"We couldn't wait, sweetie," Marianne said, enveloping her daughter in a warm hug. "The whole town's buzzing about your reopening."

Nate's gaze swept the festive decorations. "You've outdone yourself, Ginger."

"Thanks, Dad." Ginger's chest swelled with emotion. "I just hope everyone else feels the same way."

"They will," Marianne assured her, squeezing her hand. "Your resilience has inspired us all."

A cheerful voice called from the kitchen. "Ginger! Where do you want these gingerbread men?"

Cara emerged, carefully balancing a tray of cookies. Her eyes widened at the sight of the Lawrences. "Oh! Hello!"

"Perfect timing, Cara," Ginger said, grateful for her best friend's presence. "Let's set them up on the front counter."

As they arranged the cookies, Ginger whispered, "What if this is all for nothing?"

Cara paused, fixing Ginger with a determined look. "It won't be. This town loves you, Ginger. They're ready to move forward."

Ginger nodded, her friend's words bolstering her courage. She picked up a gingerbread man, inspiration striking.

"Let's make this display special," she said, positioning the cookie in a jaunty pose. "Give each one a personality."

Cara grinned, catching on. She placed another cookie with its arms outstretched. "Like this?"

"Exactly!" Ginger laughed, her earlier doubts fading. "Let's show Haversham Falls that even cookies can bounce back from adversity."

The clock struck nine, and Ginger took a deep breath. "It's time."

She strode to the front door, her heart pounding. With a quick glance at Cara, who gave her an encouraging nod, Ginger turned the sign to "Open" and swung the door wide.

A wave of excited chatter washed over her as the townsfolk poured in. Their eyes lit up at the sight of the whimsically arranged gingerbread men.

"Oh, Ginger!" Mrs. Holloway exclaimed, clasping her hands together. "They're absolutely darling!"

Ginger beamed, warmth spreading through her chest. "Thank you, Mrs. Holloway. How about a cookie to start your day?"

"I'd be delighted, dear."

As Ginger handed over a gingerbread man, she leaned in conspiratorially. "You know, this little fellow reminds me of how our town pulled together during the mystery."

Mrs. Holloway's eyes crinkled with understanding. "Indeed it does. We're stronger than ever now, aren't we?"

"Absolutely," Ginger agreed, her voice thick with emotion. She cleared her throat, turning to the next customer. "Good morning, Mr. Fitch! How are you holding up?"

The elderly man's weathered face softened. "Much better now that your shop's open again, Ginger. It's been too quiet around here."

Ginger handed him a cookie. "Well, we'll just have to make up for lost time with extra cheer, won't we?"

As she continued greeting customers, Ginger felt a renewed sense of purpose. Each smile, each shared memory of the town's resilience, reinforced her belief in the power of community.

The townspeople savored their gingerbread men, soft sighs of contentment filling the air. Mr. Fitch took a bite, his eyes widening with delight.

"Ginger, this takes me right back to my childhood!"

Ginger grinned. "That's the magic of gingerbread, isn't it?"

Mrs. Holloway nodded enthusiastically. "It's like a warm hug for the soul."

Ginger's chest swelled with pride. She'd poured her heart into these cookies, hoping to bring a taste of joy back to Haversham Falls.

"Remember the summer fair last year?" someone called out. "Ginger's booth was the talk of the town!"

A chorus of agreements rippled through the bakery. Ginger felt her cheeks flush.

"We've been through a lot," she said softly. "But look at us now."

The chatter grew, stories of shared experiences weaving through the air like the scent of spices. Ginger's eyes stung with unshed tears of happiness.

Ginger Snapped

Needing a moment, she slipped out the front door. The town square bustled with life. Laughter rang out from a group near the fountain. Two old friends embraced on a park bench.

Ginger took a deep breath, savoring the crisp air and the warmth of the sun on her face. Her heart felt full to bursting.

"We made it," she whispered to herself. "We really made it."

A tug on Ginger's apron snapped her out of her reverie. She looked down to find little Timmy Watson, his cherubic face smeared with crumbs and a gap-toothed grin.

"Miss Ginger! Miss Ginger!" Timmy bounced on his toes. "Your gingerbread men are magic!"

Ginger crouched down, her green eyes twinkling. "Oh really? And what makes them so magical?"

A cluster of children gathered around, their voices overlapping in excitement.

"Mine winked at me!"

"I swear mine did a backflip!"

"Mine tasted like Christmas morning!"

Ginger laughed, her heart swelling with joy. "Well, I'll let you in on a secret," she whispered conspiratorially. "The magic ingredient is love."

The children's eyes widened in wonder.

"Now, run along and enjoy the day," Ginger said, ruffling Timmy's hair.

As the children scampered off, Ginger noticed a shift in the atmosphere. The townsfolk were gathering near the gazebo, their faces more somber.

"It's time," she murmured to herself, straightening her apron.

Ginger made her way to the crowd, where Mayor Thompkins stood at a small podium.

"Friends," the mayor began, "we're here to remember Edith Fernwood."

A hush fell over the assembly. Ginger's mind raced with memories of the eccentric old woman who had been at the center of so much drama.

"Edith was... well, Edith was a force of nature," Mayor Thompkins continued, eliciting a few chuckles.

Mrs. Holloway raised her hand. "Remember when she convinced half the town that aliens had landed in Willow Creek?"

Laughter rippled through the crowd. Ginger smiled, recalling the wild goose chase that had ensued.

"She drove me crazy," Mr. Fitch admitted. "But you know, she also helped me find my lost cat last winter."

Ginger stepped forward, her voice soft but clear. "Edith knew everything about everyone. It was infuriating sometimes, but... she cared. In her own way, she brought us all together."

As more stories were shared, Ginger felt a bittersweet ache in her chest. Edith had been a thorn in her side, but also an undeniable part of Haversham Falls' fabric.

"She would have loved this," Ginger thought, looking around at the united community. "Well, Edith, I hope you're watching. We're stronger than ever."

Ginger felt a gentle touch on her arm. Cara stood beside her, eyes glistening.

"You did it, Ging. You brought everyone together."

Ginger shook her head. "We all did."

Detective Griffith approached, his usual stern expression softened. "Ms. Lawrence, I owe you an apology."

"Water under the bridge, Detective."

"Dan. Call me Dan."

A warmth spread through Ginger's chest. She glanced at Cara, who raised an eyebrow.

Mayor Thompkins' voice rang out. "Let's join hands, everyone. For Edith, for Haversham Falls."

The townsfolk formed a circle. Ginger found herself between Cara and Dan.

"Never thought I'd see this," Dan muttered.

Ginger squeezed his hand. "Haversham Falls is full of surprises."

As the circle tightened, Ginger felt the collective heartbeat of her community. Tears pricked her eyes.

"We're stronger together," Cara whispered.

Ginger nodded, unable to speak. In that moment, she knew they'd overcome anything.

Ginger's eyes swept across the town square, taking in the scene before her. Twinkling lights adorned the storefronts, casting a warm glow over the gathered crowd. Laughter bubbled up from various corners, punctuating the gentle hum of conversation.

"Would you look at that," Ginger murmured, her voice thick with emotion.

Cara nudged her gently. "You did this, you know."

Ginger shook her head, a small smile playing on her lips. "We all did. It's like... we're baking the perfect gingerbread. Everyone's an essential ingredient."

Detective Griffith - Dan - let out a low chuckle. "Never thought I'd hear solving a murder compared to baking cookies."

"Clearly you've never had my gingerbread men," Ginger quipped, her green eyes sparkling with mirth.

She watched as Mrs. Finch, the town librarian, threw her head back in laughter at something Mr. Peterson, the retired postman, had said. The sight warmed her heart.

"You know," Ginger mused, "I always thought Haversham Falls was special, but now..."

"Now what?" Cara prompted.

Ginger took a deep breath, the scent of cinnamon and clove from a nearby vendor's stall filling her lungs. "Now I know it's not just special. It's home. It's family."

Dan cleared his throat. "Speaking of family, your parents are heading this way."

Ginger turned to see Marianne and Nate Lawrence approaching, their faces beaming with pride.

"Oh honey," Marianne exclaimed, enveloping Ginger in a tight hug. "We're so proud of you."

As Ginger returned the embrace, she felt the last of her worries melt away. Haversham Falls had found its way back to celebration and love, and she was right where she belonged.

Epilogue
A New Batch Rising

Snow fell softly over Haversham Falls, dusting the cobbled streets like powdered sugar sifted over a warm batch of snickerdoodles. From the frosted windows of Ginger Snaps Bakery, the golden light inside cast a welcoming glow onto Main Street. The small town was already buzzing about the upcoming Winter Festival, but inside the bakery, things were unusually quiet—until the bell above the door jingled.

"Morning, Miss Lawrence," called out Millie Benson, Haversham's longtime postmistress, as she stamped the snow from her boots. "Smells like Christmas in here."

"It always does this time of year," Ginger said with a soft smile, sliding a tray of molasses crinkles into the display case.

Millie leaned in close and whispered, "I read your interview in the *Herald*. 'The Pastry Detective'—has a nice ring to it."

Ginger chuckled. "I'm not sure about that title, but I'm glad the truth's out. For Edith's sake. And for Mary's."

Millie sighed, shaking her head. "Such a shame about Mary. Never would've guessed she had it in her."

"Neither did I," Ginger said quietly, wiping her hands on her apron. "But I'm trying not to let it harden me."

"Wise of you." Millie nodded. "Don't let the world turn your sugar bitter, honey."

The bell jingled again, this time admitting Cara, bundled in a deep red coat with a knit hat pulled low over her curls. Her arm was out of the sling now, but Ginger still winced every time she saw the faint scar peeking out from her friend's sleeve.

"You're late," Ginger teased.

"Blame the snow," Cara said, shaking a dusting of it from her hat. "And Detective Broody Pants, who insists on sending 'friendly check-ins' before I leave my house."

Ginger raised a brow. "Dan? Really?"

"He texted me *Be safe* with three snowflake emojis. I think that's code for *I care but don't know how to say it.*"

"Well," Ginger said, smiling into the cupcake frosting, "he's not the only one."

Cara's eyes sparkled with amusement. "Ooooh, are we finally admitting that something's baking between you two?"

Ginger rolled her eyes. "It's complicated."

"Isn't it always?" Cara leaned on the counter. "But complicated doesn't mean bad. Just… layered. Like a croissant."

"I was going to say like a lasagna," Ginger said, laughing, "but sure. Croissant works."

Just then, the door swung open again, and Dan Griffith stepped in, brushing snow from his coat. His blue eyes swept the room, landing on Ginger.

"Ladies," he said with a nod.

"Detective," Cara replied, suddenly formal.

Dan raised an eyebrow. "Still calling me that? Even after you hacked the town archives to dig up Mary's old financials?"

Cara grinned. "What can I say? I'm a rule-bending librarian."

Dan turned to Ginger. "Got a minute?"

She wiped her hands on a towel and nodded. "Sure."

He followed her behind the counter, past trays of gingerbread men and cranberry muffins, until they reached the back room. There, the air smelled of cloves and lemon zest. Ginger leaned against the flour-dusted prep table and folded her arms.

"What's up?"

Dan rubbed the back of his neck. "I wanted to thank you. Officially. You stuck with this case, even when things got dangerous."

Ginger shrugged. "I didn't really have a choice. It was my name on the line. My bakery. My life."

"But you could've backed down," he said. "Most people would've."

She met his gaze. "I couldn't let Edith's death go unanswered. And... I couldn't let Mary's lies keep spreading."

Dan nodded, then took a deep breath. "We never really talked about what happened. After. With the knife."

Ginger's eyes drifted to her arm, where the cut had long since healed. "It's just a scar now."

"I still see it in my nightmares," Dan said quietly. "You, bleeding. Cara, on the pavement. Mary lunging."

Ginger placed a hand on his. "We survived. That's what matters."

Dan's jaw tightened, but then he let out a long breath. "You amaze me, you know that?"

Ginger's breath caught.

"You faced down a killer," he said. "And you still show up every morning to bake cinnamon rolls for people who once thought you were guilty."

"It's the only way I know how to heal," she said, voice soft. "Keep baking. Keep showing up. Keep choosing sweetness."

Dan reached into his coat and pulled out a small box tied with red string. "Early Christmas present."

Ginger raised an eyebrow. "It's not even December yet."

"Just open it."

She untied the string and lifted the lid. Inside was a custom-engraved rolling pin. The words *To the woman who rolls with the punches* were etched into the wood in delicate script.

Ginger blinked rapidly. "That's... actually perfect."

Dan smiled, then reached into his other pocket. "There's something else."

"Oh?"

He pulled out a folded sheet of paper and handed it to her. It was a zoning application.

"For what?"

"For your idea," he said. "The community kitchen expansion. I filed it on your behalf. Figured Haversham Falls could use a place for culinary classes, food drives, maybe even a seasonal market."

Ginger's eyes widened. "Dan..."

"You've given this town more than pastries, Ginger. You gave them hope. You gave me hope." He hesitated. "I just wanted to give something back."

Ginger reached for his hand, squeezing it. "You already have."

They stood there for a long moment, surrounded by trays of cookies and the hum of the industrial fridge. Snow tapped softly at the windows.

Finally, Ginger smiled. "So… are you staying for dinner tonight?"

Dan's smile returned. "Only if it comes with your famous butternut squash risotto."

"And you help with the dishes."

He mock-groaned. "I knew there was a catch."

Back in the front of the bakery, Cara was directing a group of volunteers decorating gingerbread house kits for the Winter Festival. A few children were gathered at a craft table, frosting everywhere, their laughter rising above the soft instrumental carols playing on the stereo.

"Looks like we've got a full house," Dan said as they rejoined the crowd.

"Always room for more," Ginger replied, stepping behind the counter again.

As the day unfolded, Ginger moved between customers with ease—laughing, listening, frosting cookies, pouring cocoa. The buzz of gossip had shifted from murder to merriment. There were whispers about her and Dan, of course, but none with the sharp edge of suspicion anymore. Now it was all twinkling lights and cinnamon dreams.

Later that night, when the last customer had left and Cara had gone home to soak her arm, Ginger stood in the quiet of her kitchen. The last gingerbread batch of the evening was cooling. She reached for her grandmother's recipe book and flipped it open to the back—where tucked between the worn pages was a new addition: a letter to herself.

Dear Ginger,

You were never meant to just bake. You were meant to rise.

She folded the letter again and slid it behind her favorite cookie recipe.

The door creaked, and Dan poked his head in. "Ready to head out?"

Ginger nodded, turning off the lights one by one. As they stepped into the snow-kissed night, Dan offered his arm. She took it, and together they walked down Main Street beneath the glowing string lights and wreaths that adorned each lamppost.

The murder had been solved. The lies exposed. And yet, this wasn't the end.

It was only the beginning.

A new chapter.

A new recipe.

A new life—still messy, still uncertain, but finally sweet again.

GINGER'S RECIPES

1. Peppermint Mocha Cupcakes

Ingredients:

For the cupcakes:

- 1 cup all-purpose flour
- ½ cup unsweetened cocoa powder
- 1 tsp baking powder
- ½ tsp baking soda
- ¼ tsp salt
- ½ cup granulated sugar
- ½ cup brown sugar
- ½ cup vegetable oil
- 2 large eggs
- ½ cup brewed espresso or strong coffee
- ½ cup buttermilk
- 1 tsp peppermint extract
- 1 tsp vanilla extract

For the frosting:

- 1 cup unsalted butter, softened
- 3 cups powdered sugar
- 2 tbsp heavy cream
- ½ tsp peppermint extract
- Crushed candy canes for topping

Instructions:

1. Preheat oven to 350°F (175°C). Line a muffin tin with cupcake liners.
2. In a bowl, sift together flour, cocoa powder, baking powder, baking soda, and salt.
3. In another bowl, mix sugars, oil, and eggs until well combined.
4. Add espresso, buttermilk, peppermint, and vanilla extracts.
5. Gradually mix in the dry ingredients until smooth.
6. Divide batter into cupcake liners and bake 18–20 minutes. Cool completely.
7. For the frosting, beat butter until fluffy. Add powdered sugar, cream, and peppermint.
8. Pipe frosting on cooled cupcakes and top with crushed candy canes.

2. Gingerbread Snowflake Cookies

Ingredients:

- 3 cups all-purpose flour
- ¾ cup packed brown sugar
- ¾ cup molasses
- 1 large egg
- ½ cup unsalted butter, softened
- 1 tsp baking soda
- 1 tbsp ground ginger
- 1 tbsp ground cinnamon
- ½ tsp cloves
- ½ tsp nutmeg
- ½ tsp salt

For decorating:

- Royal icing or vanilla glaze
- White sprinkles or edible glitter (optional)

Instructions:

1. Beat butter and brown sugar until fluffy. Add egg and molasses and mix.
2. In a separate bowl, whisk dry ingredients. Gradually add to wet mixture.

3. Divide dough in half, flatten into discs, wrap in plastic, and chill 1 hour.

4. Preheat oven to 350°F. Roll out dough to ¼ inch. Cut snowflake shapes.

5. Bake on parchment-lined sheet for 8–10 minutes. Cool before icing.

6. Decorate with royal icing and sprinkles once completely cooled.

3. Cranberry Orange Scones

Ingredients:

- 2 cups all-purpose flour
- ½ cup sugar
- 1 tbsp baking powder
- ½ tsp salt
- Zest of 1 orange
- ½ cup cold unsalted butter, cut into cubes
- ½ cup dried cranberries
- ⅔ cup heavy cream
- 1 large egg
- 1 tsp vanilla extract

For the glaze:

- ½ cup powdered sugar
- 1 tbsp orange juice

Instructions:

1. Preheat oven to 400°F (205°C).
2. Mix flour, sugar, baking powder, salt, and orange zest in a large bowl.

3. Cut in butter with a pastry cutter or fingers until coarse crumbs form.

4. Stir in cranberries.

5. In a separate bowl, whisk cream, egg, and vanilla. Add to flour mixture.

6. Mix gently until dough forms. Pat into a circle and cut into 8 wedges.

7. Place on baking sheet and bake 15–18 minutes.

8. Mix powdered sugar and orange juice for glaze. Drizzle over cooled scones.

4. Eggnog Cream Pie

Ingredients:

For the crust:

- 1½ cups graham cracker crumbs
- ¼ cup granulated sugar
- 6 tbsp unsalted butter, melted

For the filling:

- 2 cups eggnog
- 1 cup heavy cream
- ⅓ cup cornstarch
- ½ cup granulated sugar
- ¼ tsp ground nutmeg
- ½ tsp cinnamon
- Pinch of salt
- 2 tbsp unsalted butter
- 1 tsp vanilla extract

Topping:

- Whipped cream and extra nutmeg

Instructions:

1. Preheat oven to 350°F. Mix crust ingredients and press into 9-inch pie pan.
2. Bake crust for 8 minutes, then cool.
3. For filling, whisk eggnog, cream, cornstarch, sugar, spices, and salt in saucepan.
4. Cook over medium heat until thickened, stirring constantly (8–10 minutes).
5. Remove from heat and stir in butter and vanilla.
6. Pour into crust and chill at least 4 hours.
7. Top with whipped cream and a dusting of nutmeg before serving.

5. Hot Cocoa Brownie Bites

Ingredients:

- ½ cup unsalted butter
- 1 cup granulated sugar
- 2 large eggs
- 1 tsp vanilla extract
- ⅓ cup unsweetened cocoa powder
- ½ cup all-purpose flour
- ¼ tsp salt
- ¼ tsp baking powder

Topping:

- Mini marshmallows
- Melted chocolate for drizzle

Instructions:

1. Preheat oven to 350°F. Grease a mini muffin tin.
2. Melt butter and whisk in sugar, eggs, and vanilla.
3. Stir in cocoa, flour, salt, and baking powder.
4. Spoon into muffin tin and bake 12–14 minutes.
5. Top each with 3 mini marshmallows and broil for 30 seconds until toasted.

6. Drizzle melted chocolate over cooled brownie bites.

6. Cinnamon Star Bread

Ingredients:

Dough:

- 2¼ tsp active dry yeast
- ¾ cup warm milk (110°F)
- ¼ cup granulated sugar
- 2¾ cups all-purpose flour
- ¼ tsp salt
- 1 large egg
- ¼ cup unsalted butter, softened

Filling:

- ¼ cup unsalted butter, melted
- ½ cup brown sugar
- 1 tbsp ground cinnamon

Instructions:

1. Dissolve yeast in warm milk with 1 tbsp sugar. Let sit 10 minutes until foamy.
2. Mix flour, remaining sugar, and salt. Add egg, butter, and yeast mixture. Knead until smooth.
3. Cover and let rise 1 hour.

4. Divide dough into 4 equal pieces. Roll each into a 10-inch circle.

5. Place one circle on a baking sheet. Brush with melted butter, sprinkle cinnamon sugar. Repeat with next 2 layers. Top with the final circle.

6. Place a small cup in the center. Cut dough into 16 equal sections, leaving center intact. Twist each pair outward twice and pinch ends together.

7. Let rise 20 minutes. Preheat oven to 375°F.

8. Bake for 20–25 minutes until golden. Dust with powdered sugar if desired.

7. White Chocolate Cranberry Biscotti

Ingredients:

- 2 cups all-purpose flour
- 1 tsp baking powder
- ¼ tsp salt
- ½ cup unsalted butter, softened
- ¾ cup sugar
- 2 large eggs
- 1 tsp vanilla extract
- ½ cup dried cranberries
- ½ cup chopped white chocolate (plus more for drizzling)

Instructions:

1. Preheat oven to 350°F. Line baking sheet with parchment.
2. Cream butter and sugar. Add eggs one at a time, then vanilla.
3. Mix flour, baking powder, and salt. Add to butter mixture. Stir in cranberries and white chocolate.
4. Divide dough in half. Shape into two logs (12x2 inches).
5. Bake 25 minutes. Let cool 10 minutes, then slice diagonally into ¾-inch pieces.
6. Lay slices flat and bake 10 minutes per side. Cool completely.

7. Drizzle with melted white chocolate if desired.

8. Sticky Toffee Pudding with Bourbon Sauce

Ingredients:

Pudding:

- 1 cup chopped dates
- 1 tsp baking soda
- 1 cup boiling water
- ½ cup brown sugar
- ¼ cup butter, softened
- 2 large eggs
- 1 tsp vanilla extract
- 1¼ cups flour
- 1 tsp baking powder
- Pinch of salt

Sauce:

- ½ cup butter
- 1 cup brown sugar
- ½ cup heavy cream
- 2 tbsp bourbon (optional)

Instructions:

1. Preheat oven to 350°F. Grease a baking dish.

2. Combine dates, baking soda, and boiling water. Let sit 10 minutes.

3. Cream butter and sugar. Add eggs and vanilla. Stir in date mixture.

4. Add flour, baking powder, and salt. Mix until just combined.

5. Pour into dish. Bake 30–35 minutes.

6. For sauce, simmer butter, brown sugar, and cream for 5 minutes. Stir in bourbon.

7. Serve pudding warm, drenched in sauce.

9. Snowball Coconut Macaroons

Ingredients:

- 3 cups sweetened shredded coconut
- ¾ cup sweetened condensed milk
- 1 tsp vanilla extract
- 1 large egg white
- Pinch of salt
- Powdered sugar (for dusting)

Instructions:

1. Preheat oven to 325°F. Line baking sheet with parchment.

2. Combine coconut, condensed milk, and vanilla.

3. Beat egg white with salt until stiff peaks form. Fold into coconut mixture.

Ginger Snapped

4. Scoop into balls and place on sheet.
5. Bake 20–25 minutes until golden. Cool and dust with powdered sugar.

10. Chocolate Peppermint Bark

Ingredients:

- 12 oz dark chocolate chips
- 12 oz white chocolate chips
- 1 tsp peppermint extract
- ½ cup crushed candy canes

Instructions:

1. Melt dark chocolate. Stir in half of the peppermint extract. Spread on parchment-lined tray. Chill 10 minutes.
2. Melt white chocolate. Stir in remaining peppermint extract. Spread over dark layer.
3. Sprinkle with crushed candy canes. Chill until firm.
4. Break into shards and store in a tin.

11. Christmas Tree Sugar Cookie Stacks

Ingredients:

- 3 cups all-purpose flour
- 1 tsp baking powder
- ½ tsp salt
- 1 cup butter, softened
- 1 cup sugar
- 1 large egg
- 1 tsp vanilla extract
- Green food coloring
- Buttercream frosting (for stacking)
- Sprinkles and star candies

Instructions:

1. Preheat oven to 350°F. Cream butter and sugar. Add egg, vanilla, and green food coloring.
2. Stir in flour, baking powder, and salt. Chill dough 30 minutes.
3. Roll and cut various sizes of stars. Bake 8–10 minutes.
4. Stack with frosting, largest to smallest. Decorate with sprinkles and top with a star.

12. Spiced Apple Cider Donuts

Ingredients:

- 1½ cups all-purpose flour
- ½ cup sugar
- 1 tsp baking powder
- ½ tsp cinnamon
- ¼ tsp nutmeg
- ¼ tsp salt
- 1 large egg
- ½ cup apple cider (reduced to ¼ cup)
- ¼ cup milk
- 2 tbsp butter, melted

Instructions:

1. Preheat oven to 350°F. Grease donut pan.
2. Reduce ½ cup cider to ¼ cup over medium heat.
3. Mix dry ingredients. In another bowl, whisk egg, cider, milk, and butter. Combine.
4. Fill donut pan and bake 10–12 minutes.
5. Roll warm donuts in cinnamon sugar.

13. Holiday Fudge Wreath

Ingredients:

- 3 cups semi-sweet chocolate chips
- 1 can (14 oz) sweetened condensed milk
- ¼ cup butter
- 1 tsp vanilla extract
- ½ cup chopped walnuts (optional)
- ½ cup red and green M&Ms or dried cranberries

Instructions:

1. Melt chocolate, milk, and butter over low heat. Stir until smooth.
2. Add vanilla and nuts. Pour into a greased bundt or ring mold.
3. Top with candy and chill 2+ hours. Slice into wedges to serve.

14. Brown Butter Pecan Shortbread

Ingredients:

- 1 cup unsalted butter
- ½ cup powdered sugar
- 1 tsp vanilla extract
- 2 cups all-purpose flour
- ½ cup chopped pecans
- Pinch of salt

Instructions:

1. Brown butter in a pan, then chill until soft.
2. Cream butter and sugar. Add vanilla, flour, salt, and pecans.
3. Roll into a log and chill. Slice and bake at 325°F for 12–15 minutes.
4. Dust with extra powdered sugar.

15. Chocolate-Dipped Orange Peel

Ingredients:

- Peels from 3 large oranges
- 1 cup sugar
- ½ cup water
- 6 oz dark chocolate, melted

Instructions:

1. Slice orange peels into strips. Boil in water 3 times to reduce bitterness.
2. Simmer sugar and water. Add peels and simmer 30 minutes.
3. Dry on rack overnight.
4. Dip in melted chocolate. Chill until set.

🎄 DIY Christmas Projects: Full Instructions

1. Mason Jar Snow Globes

You'll Need:

- Mason jars with lids
- Waterproof figurines (trees, snowmen, deer)
- Glycerin
- Distilled water
- Glitter
- Hot glue gun

Instructions:

1. Glue the figurines to the inside of the jar lid using a hot glue gun. Let dry completely.
2. Fill the jar almost to the top with distilled water.
3. Add a few drops of glycerin (to slow the glitter's fall) and about 1 tsp glitter.
4. Screw the lid on tightly with the figurines upside down inside the jar.
5. Seal the edges with hot glue to prevent leaks.
6. Turn upside down and shake to watch your snow globe sparkle!

2. Cinnamon Stick Candle Holders

You'll Need:

- Glass votive holders or small jars
- Cinnamon sticks (roughly the same height as the votive)
- Twine or holiday ribbon
- Hot glue gun
- Tea lights or votive candles

Instructions:

1. Apply a line of hot glue vertically to each cinnamon stick.
2. Press each stick upright against the glass votive holder until fully surrounded.
3. Wrap with rustic twine or festive ribbon and tie into a bow.
4. Place a candle inside and light. The warmth will release a subtle cinnamon scent.

3. Dried Orange Garland

You'll Need:

- 3–4 oranges
- Knife
- Baking sheet and parchment paper
- Twine
- Needle or mini clothespins
- Optional: cranberries, cinnamon sticks

Instructions:

1. Slice oranges into ¼-inch thick rounds.
2. Blot slices with paper towels to remove moisture.
3. Arrange on parchment-lined baking sheet.
4. Bake at 200°F for 2–3 hours, flipping every 30 minutes, until dry and leathery.
5. Thread twine through each slice (use a needle or clothespins).
6. Add cranberries or cinnamon sticks between slices for extra charm.

4. Book Page Ornaments
You'll Need:

- Old book pages
- Scissors
- Glue or Mod Podge
- String or ornament hooks
- Optional: glitter, small buttons, ribbon

Instructions:

1. Cut book pages into strips or shapes (stars, snowflakes, trees).
2. Fold or layer as desired and glue shapes together.
3. Add a ribbon or looped string to hang.
4. Brush edges with Mod Podge and sprinkle with glitter for sparkle.

5. Peppermint Bark Gift Jars

You'll Need:

- Mason jars
- ½ cup crushed candy canes
- ½ cup white chocolate chips
- ½ cup dark chocolate chips
- Decorative ribbon and gift tags

Instructions:

1. Layer chocolate chips and crushed candy canes in jars.
2. Write instructions on the tag:
   "Melt all contents in a bowl over low heat. Pour onto parchment paper, spread thin, and chill. Break into pieces."
3. Seal jar, tie with ribbon and tag, and gift to friends and neighbors.

6. Pinecone Fire Starters

You'll Need:

- Pinecones
- Beeswax or soy wax
- Candle wicks or cotton string
- Muffin tin and paper liners
- Optional: cinnamon oil or dried herbs

Instructions:

1. Line muffin tins with paper liners and place a pinecone in each.
2. Melt wax over low heat and add a few drops of essential oil if desired.
3. Pour wax into each liner until it covers half the pinecone.
4. Let cool. Trim the wick (or tuck string between scales).
5. Package in cellophane with a festive tag.

7. Sock Snowmen

You'll Need:

- White crew socks
- Rice or beans
- Rubber bands
- Buttons, fabric scraps, googly eyes, felt, ribbon
- Hot glue

Instructions:

1. Cut sock at the heel. Use the foot part.
2. Turn inside out, tie off bottom with rubber band, and flip back.
3. Fill sock with rice for weight and shape.
4. Tie again to separate "head" and "body."
5. Decorate with buttons, a felt nose, scarf, and eyes.
6. Use top part of sock as a beanie hat!

8. Mini Wreath Place Cards

You'll Need:

- Fresh rosemary or faux greenery
- Twine or thin floral wire
- Name tags or kraft paper
- Hot glue gun
- Mini pinecones, berries, or buttons (optional)

Instructions:

1. Shape sprigs of rosemary into a 3-inch circle and secure ends with twine or wire.
2. Attach name tags with glue or punch holes to tie.
3. Embellish with tiny pinecones or faux berries for flair.
4. Set one at each holiday place setting.

9. Hot Cocoa Kit Ornaments

You'll Need:

- Clear plastic ball ornaments with a removable top
- Hot cocoa mix
- Mini marshmallows
- Crushed peppermint, mini chocolate chips
- Funnel

Instructions:

1. Remove ornament tops and insert funnel.
2. Pour in 2 tbsp cocoa mix, followed by layers of toppings.
3. Replace top and shake gently to settle.
4. Tie ribbon around top and add a tag:
   "Empty into a mug, add 8 oz hot milk, stir & enjoy!"

10. Fabric Scrap Trees

You'll Need:

- Cardboard or poster board
- Hot glue gun
- Fabric scraps in green, red, and gold
- Buttons, sequins, or ribbon
- Scissors

Instructions:

1. Cut cardboard into triangle tree shapes (6–8 inches tall).
2. Tear or cut fabric into strips.
3. Glue strips from bottom to top, overlapping like shingles.
4. Trim sides to follow triangle shape.
5. Add buttons as "ornaments" and top with a fabric or felt star.

🍽 CHRISTMAS DINNER RECIPES & SIDES

1. Herb-Crusted Prime Rib Roast

Sides: Garlic Mashed Potatoes & Honey-Glazed Carrots

Ingredients (Main):

- 1 (5 lb) prime rib roast
- ¼ cup olive oil
- 1 tbsp salt
- 1 tbsp black pepper
- 1 tbsp fresh rosemary, chopped
- 1 tbsp thyme, chopped
- 6 garlic cloves, minced

Instructions:

1. Preheat oven to 450°F.
2. Pat roast dry. Mix olive oil, herbs, garlic, salt, and pepper into a paste. Rub generously over roast.
3. Place roast in a roasting pan bone-side down. Bake 20 minutes, then reduce heat to 325°F.
4. Continue roasting for 90–120 minutes until internal temp reaches 130°F (medium rare).

5. Let rest 20 minutes before slicing.

Garlic Mashed Potatoes:

- Boil 3 lbs Yukon gold potatoes.
- Mash with 1 stick butter, 1 cup warm heavy cream, and 4 roasted garlic cloves.
- Season with salt and pepper.

Honey-Glazed Carrots:

- Roast 1½ lbs baby carrots with 2 tbsp honey, 2 tbsp butter, and a pinch of cinnamon at 375°F for 25 minutes.

2. Brown Sugar Glazed Ham
Sides: Scalloped Potatoes & Bacon Brussels Sprouts
Ingredients (Main):
- 1 spiral-cut ham (7–8 lbs)
- 1 cup brown sugar
- ¼ cup Dijon mustard
- ½ tsp ground cloves
- ½ cup orange juice

Instructions:
1. Preheat oven to 325°F. Place ham in roasting pan.
2. Mix brown sugar, mustard, cloves, and juice.
3. Brush over ham, cover with foil, and bake 90 minutes.
4. Uncover, baste again, and bake 30 more minutes until caramelized.

Scalloped Potatoes:
- Layer thinly sliced potatoes and onion in a baking dish.
- Pour over 2 cups cream mixed with salt, pepper, garlic, and 1 cup shredded Gruyère.
- Bake at 375°F for 45–50 minutes.

Bacon Brussels Sprouts:
- Halve 1 lb Brussels sprouts.

Ginger Snapped

- Sauté in a skillet with 4 chopped bacon slices until golden.
- Finish with a splash of balsamic vinegar.

3. Cranberry-Stuffed Turkey Breast

Sides: Wild Rice Pilaf & Roasted Butternut Squash

Ingredients (Main):

- 1 whole boneless turkey breast (3–4 lbs)
- 1 cup prepared cranberry sauce
- 1½ cups stuffing (cornbread or traditional)
- 2 tbsp olive oil
- Salt and pepper

Instructions:

1. Butterfly turkey breast and pound flat.
2. Spread cranberry sauce and stuffing over meat. Roll and tie with kitchen twine.
3. Rub with oil, salt, and pepper.
4. Roast at 350°F for 1 hour 15 minutes, or until 165°F internal temp. Rest 10 minutes before slicing.

Wild Rice Pilaf:

- Sauté ½ cup chopped onion and 1 carrot in butter.
- Add 1½ cups wild rice mix, 3 cups broth, and simmer 40 minutes. Stir in ¼ cup slivered almonds.

Roasted Butternut Squash:

- Toss cubed squash with olive oil, salt, pepper, and maple syrup.
- Roast at 400°F for 30 minutes until caramelized.

4. Apple Cider Pork Tenderloin

Sides: Sweet Potato Gratin & Cider-Braised Cabbage

Ingredients (Main):

- 2 pork tenderloins (about 1.5 lbs each)
- 1½ cups apple cider
- 2 tbsp Dijon mustard
- 1 tbsp thyme
- Salt and pepper

Instructions:

1. Marinate pork in cider, mustard, thyme, salt, and pepper for 4 hours.
2. Sear in a hot skillet, then transfer to oven at 400°F for 20 minutes.
3. Let rest, slice, and drizzle with reduced marinade.

Sweet Potato Gratin:

- Layer thinly sliced sweet potatoes with cream, garlic, and a touch of nutmeg.
- Top with Parmesan. Bake at 375°F for 40 minutes.

Cider-Braised Cabbage:

- Cook ½ head sliced red cabbage in 1 cup apple cider, 2 tbsp vinegar, and 1 tbsp brown sugar for 30 minutes.

5. Garlic & Herb Roasted Chicken
Sides: Parmesan Green Beans & Sour Cream Mashed Potatoes
Ingredients (Main):

- 1 whole chicken (4–5 lbs)
- 2 tbsp olive oil
- 1 lemon, halved
- 4 garlic cloves, smashed
- Fresh rosemary, thyme, salt, and pepper

Instructions:

1. Preheat oven to 375°F. Stuff chicken with lemon, garlic, and herbs.
2. Rub skin with oil, salt, and pepper.
3. Roast 1 hour 20 minutes or until juices run clear.

Parmesan Green Beans:

- Steam green beans, then sauté in butter and garlic.
- Toss with grated Parmesan.

Sour Cream Mashed Potatoes:

- Mash cooked potatoes with butter, sour cream, and a dash of milk.
- Season with salt and chives.

6. Mushroom Wellington (Vegetarian)
Sides: Crispy Roast Potatoes & Maple-Roasted Carrots

Ingredients (Main):

- 2 tbsp butter
- 1½ lbs mixed mushrooms, chopped
- 1 small onion, diced
- 2 cloves garlic
- 2 tbsp Dijon mustard
- 1 sheet puff pastry
- 1 egg, for brushing

Instructions:

1. Sauté mushrooms, onion, and garlic in butter until browned. Stir in mustard and let cool.
2. Roll out puff pastry, place filling in center, fold and seal.
3. Brush with egg and bake at 400°F for 35 minutes until golden.

Crispy Roast Potatoes:

- Boil halved Yukon gold potatoes for 10 minutes.
- Roast with oil, rosemary, and salt at 425°F until crisp.

Maple-Roasted Carrots:

- Toss carrots in maple syrup, butter, and thyme. Roast at 375°F for 30–35 minutes.

7. Maple-Dijon Glazed Salmon

Sides: Herbed Couscous & Lemon Asparagus

Ingredients (Main):

- 4 salmon fillets
- 2 tbsp maple syrup
- 1 tbsp Dijon mustard
- 1 tbsp soy sauce
- Salt and pepper

Instructions:

1. Mix glaze ingredients. Brush on salmon.
2. Bake at 400°F for 12–15 minutes.

Herbed Couscous:

- Cook couscous in broth. Fluff with fork and stir in parsley, lemon zest, and olive oil.

Lemon Asparagus:

- Roast asparagus with olive oil and lemon slices at 375°F for 15 minutes.

8. Cranberry Orange Glazed Duck

Sides: Garlic Fingerlings & Red Wine-Poached Pears

Ingredients (Main):

- 1 whole duck (4–5 lbs)
- Salt and pepper
- 1 cup cranberry sauce
- ½ cup orange juice
- 2 tbsp honey

Instructions:

1. Score duck skin. Season and roast at 375°F for 1½–2 hours.
2. Simmer cranberry, juice, and honey to make glaze. Brush onto duck during last 30 minutes.

Garlic Fingerlings:

- Roast fingerling potatoes with garlic cloves and rosemary until crispy.

Red Wine-Poached Pears:

- Simmer peeled pears in red wine, sugar, cinnamon, and cloves until tender.

9. Stuffed Acorn Squash (Vegetarian)
Sides: Pomegranate Arugula Salad & Sourdough Bread

Ingredients (Main):
- 2 acorn squash, halved and roasted
- 1 tbsp olive oil
- 1 cup cooked farro or quinoa
- ½ cup sautéed mushrooms
- ¼ cup chopped chestnuts
- Dried cranberries, thyme, and sage

Instructions:
1. Roast squash at 400°F for 30 minutes.
2. Mix grains, mushrooms, chestnuts, and herbs.
3. Stuff squash and bake 15 minutes more.

Arugula Salad:
- Toss arugula with pomegranate seeds, feta, and balsamic vinaigrette.

Sourdough Bread:
- Warm sourdough slices, brush with herbed butter.

10. Classic Ricotta Lasagna

Sides: Caesar Salad & Rosemary Focaccia

Ingredients (Main):

- 9 cooked lasagna noodles
- 2 cups ricotta cheese
- 1 egg
- 2 cups shredded mozzarella
- 2½ cups marinara sauce
- 1 tsp basil, 1 tsp oregano
- Grated Parmesan

Instructions:

1. Mix ricotta, egg, herbs, and ½ cup mozzarella.
2. Layer sauce, noodles, ricotta mix, more sauce, and mozzarella.
3. Repeat layers, top with Parmesan.
4. Bake at 375°F for 40 minutes.

Caesar Salad:

- Toss romaine with Caesar dressing, croutons, and shaved Parmesan.

Rosemary Focaccia:

- Make or buy focaccia. Reheat and brush with olive oil and chopped rosemary.

Meet Patti

Meet Patti, the creative force behind "Where the Magic Happens." More than just an author, Patti brings stories to life as the Executive Producer of an animated TV series based on her heartwarming tale "ELLIOT FINDS A HOME"—the story of a special dog with thumbs and his silent friend who prove that sometimes, actions speak louder than words.

Patti's writing journey has been nothing short of remarkable. A cherished author at Polygon Entertainment, she's danced her way onto the USA TODAY bestseller list and claimed Amazon's #1 spot multiple times. With 7 dozen books spanning from Urban Fantasy to Horror, Patti weaves tales that transport readers to worlds limited only by imagination.

Her life reads like an adventure novel filled with fascinating chapters:

At just 4 years old, she charmed audiences on "Romper Room" She shared memorable moments with Captain Kangaroo and Mr. Green Jeans She once enjoyed a train ride and sandwich with Sidney Poitier She high-fived President Nixon during a circus visit She attended school alongside magician David Copperfield She roller-skated with John Travolta before his rise to fame She warmed her hands and heart sharing cocoa with Abe Vigoda

When she's not crafting bestsellers, Patti embraces life as a teacher, grandmother, and devoted pet parent. Known affectionately as the "Queen of Halloween," this Wiccan High Priestess infuses her spooky stories with authentic magic that keeps readers spellbound.

Patti's books fly off shelves as quickly as they're stocked, so follow her social media to stay connected with this one-of-a-kind storyteller whose magical worlds welcome all who dare to dream.

www.ingramcontent.com/pod-product-compliance
Lightning Source LLC
LaVergne TN
LVHW041814060526
838201LV00046B/1268